IT TAKES

ALSO BY THE AUTHOR

The Girl in 402
A paranormal horror novella

Black Eyed Susan
A cosmic horror novel

IT TAKES

A.W. SCHOFIELD

PUBLISHED BY: A.W. SCHOFIELD

All rights reserved. No part of this publication may be reproduced, distributed, or transmitted in any form or by any means without the prior written permission of the publisher, except for use of quotations in a book review.

The story, all names, characters, and incidents portrayed in this text are works of fiction. No identification with actual persons (living or deceased), places, buildings, and products is intended or should be inferred.

Copyright © 2025 A.W. Schofield

Published by A.W. Schofield

Cover by A.W. Schofield

First Edition. October 2025.

For Jess,
because we're still here.

Content Warning: This book contains depictions of and/or references to domestic violence, murder, child murder, self harm, mental illness, and suicide.

If you have been having suicidal thoughts, please reach out to someone. The world is better with you in it.

Last night I saw upon the stair,
A little man who wasn't there,
He wasn't there again today,
Oh, how I wish he'd go away...

—*William Hughes Mearns, "Antigonish"*

PROLOGUE

THE FOUR WORDS

"Are you sitting down?"

I didn't know why, but at first I thought that would mean what was coming next was a good thing. Then I remembered.

"He's gone?" I said, somewhere between a question and a confirmation.

"I'm sorry Maddy."

I took in a deep breath and cleared my throat, "It's okay. Thank you."

I hung up and I waited… waited for it to hit. But that's the thing they don't tell you about grief, it doesn't work on your time. My mind stayed in the moment. Never allowing itself to falter or drift back to the memories. Instead I just thought about how I was going to tell Sammy.

IT TAKES

He cried right away. Hearing him sob over the phone hurt worse than anything, but still my mind wouldn't allow me to feel it all. Still the dam wouldn't burst.

I sat and stared at old pictures. I stared and I waited for the switch to flip. I wanted to feel it. He deserved to be grieved properly, and I knew I had it in me. But, nothing. It didn't click. Maybe I prepared myself too well.

It wasn't until we got to the house... That damn old house in the woods where I spent the first 19 odd years of my life. Then my brain had nowhere to run.

I excused myself to the tiny old bathroom down the hall. Once barricaded inside, I stood in front of the sink with the cracked mirror, and turned on the faucet to cover all the sounds that were rapidly escaping me.

It wasn't just the house that got me. It was all the little things. The little trinkets, the pictures, the oddities. Those little slices of home that sat in the same spot for my whole life, now being taken away to be repurposed. In their place, just a little shape cut out from the dust—waiting to be filled in by something new. Something that wasn't my dad anymore.

We took inventory of all he left behind. There was no money, no inheritance, and few noteworthy possessions. Unsurprising, as we never had much to begin with. All that was really left of him was in our memories. That, and a book.

A.W. SCHOFIELD

I found it tucked away in the drawer of his nightstand. A manuscript. Completed, but never published.

Dad wrote true crime mostly. The occasional thriller. They never became much of anything, and he mostly gave up on it after Sammy and I came along. After that, there was always something in the way.

I knew he wrote about what happened. He didn't keep it a secret, but I never found out that he finished it. Whether it was before or after he got sick, I didn't know. He asked us not to read it, and not to think about it. We weren't keen to.

Much of what happened back in the winter of 2015 was lost on me. I knew lots of pieces, but they never fit together, and dad wouldn't talk about them. He always insisted that we move on.

I knew about the basement—I saw it. I knew about the voices—I heard them. I remember being afraid. I remember The Sharp Man. I remember when Sammy disappeared. But how it ended? What it all meant? That I never knew.

After 10 years your brain tries to coat those memories with rationales. I did my best. I almost convinced myself it was all explainable. Then this stack of papers got in my hands.

It was a long time before I decided to sit down and read it. I couldn't bear a snapshot into a life that didn't exist anymore. But given everything that happened, I knew I had to. For my closure and, more importantly, for his memory.

IT TAKES

I sat at my desk as the wind howled and snow cascaded outside my bedroom window. The only source of light was my desk lamp, its orange glow saturated the pages.

I steadied myself, peeling up the lower right corner of the completely blank front page, and then I turned it.

The following page read merely two words.

A.W. SCHOFIELD

IT TAKES

A.W. SCHOFIELD

IT TAKES

IT TAKES

CHAPTER I

MEMENTO

"Are you sitting down?" Maddy shouted from her room.

The divot on the right couch cushion molded to my form and clung to me like a needy pet.

"...Yeah?" I grumbled.

"I left my pop on the coffee table, can you bring it to me?"

I grunted, "You're killing me."

"I'm in a game, dad, I can't leave right now."

"Well I'm watching..." What the fuck was I watching? "Okay fine."

I rocked my tired body back and forth, gaining enough momentum to eventually escape the leather quicksand.

I left the cold glow of the TV, bottle of Baja Blast in hand, and made my way through the living room.

Didn't bother with the lights, I could do this in the dark. I could do it in my sleep at this point.

IT TAKES

The layout of the house was simple. Single story. Living room and kitchen laid out fairly open concept.

All of the rooms—the three bedrooms, single bathroom, and door to the basement—laid tucked away in a long, narrow 7-shaped hallway beginning at the far end of the right wall. And that was all there was to it.

It was rugged, it was small, it was frankly a glorified cabin in the woods, but it was ours.

Our driveway rested amongst a dense line of trees, easy to miss, off a long dirt road. The nearest neighbour was a 30-minute hike down that road. I never met them. Even more trees surrounded our property. The woods behind our house stretched on for kilometers. Our own little slice of wilderness.

"Here you go, freak." I said, slamming the drink hard on her desk because she looked a little too concentrated.

She jumped. I won.

"Thanks."

"Are you winning?" I asked, deliberately being a bother.

"Well there's no 'winning', dad."

"What?"

"It's like a... farming game."

"Farming..."

"Yeah. You have a ranch and crops and you gotta—"

"You couldn't take a break from *farming* to get your own drink?"

"Well I was in the cave."

"Why were you farming in a cave?"

"Dad... Go away. Thank you. Go away."

"Freak."

I lurched back down the long hallway, taking a brief detour to make sure Sammy was still asleep. I knew he was, I would hear it if he wasn't, but I still always had to check.

After that unnecessary confirmation, I went back to my spot in front of the big TV. I didn't even really care about what was on it most of the time, it was just what I did. My comfort, my place.

When you live somewhere long enough, it becomes so much more than shelter and a sanctuary. It becomes memory. Memory given dimension. Every room filled with chapters of your story.

Depending on the memories, it can be a blessing or a curse. Sometimes it can be both at the same time.

After 17 years, you build up a whole lot of both.

There's pain, heartache, regret, and grief etched into the texture on every wall. The hardest times of my life—of all our lives—lingering ever present like the dust you sweep away but always comes back. Yet despite that, there's not a second I would want to forget.

I can look at my bed and see the empty space where Steph used to lay—the last spot I saw her in before she left; but I can also look at the spot next to the coffee table and see where Sammy took his first steps. That's worth all the heartache in the world.

***

IT TAKES

We kept up with the house okay, we did what we had to, we could even make it look presentable sometimes—and that's where the basement came in handy.

Our basement was unfinished. There was really nothing to it. Just a big open space with a cold concrete floor. Wooden beams and insulation patterned the walls and ceilings. It was freezing, it smelled, it was dark, and we just didn't go down there much. It became a place to haphazardly store all the stuff we weren't using but didn't want to get rid of.

I thought about getting it finished, but I never had the money. Then I didn't have the money or the time. The two of us raising one kid was hard; me raising two kids alone was objectively impossible. But that's what you do when you're a parent. You hurt, you cry, you reach your limit, you go insane, and then you do it.

***

Maddy was all grown up now, independent and doing well. I always knew she would be okay. My biggest concern was next summer when she'd turn 18. She never said it, but I knew she would be gone not long after.

Sammy was doing okay too, relatively. At 5 years old he was finally developing into an actual human being and not just a screaming badger.

Because of this I was able to work more hours and not have to budget for a babysitter which was huge. We were in a nice period of calm and relative stability. Something I didn't know I could value this much. But some things aren't meant to last.

IT TAKES

CHAPTER II

WHISPER MEN

I didn't believe in ghosts. I didn't believe in demons or haunted houses, and in the 17 years I lived here, I was never challenged on that.

The house creaked, like any old house. There were noises, but none that wouldn't be expected from living so close to the woods. We got critters, not ghosts. I doubt we would even be able to hear anything a ghost would do over the crickets and cicadas.

Winter was different though. All those noises went away. It could be eerie, the silence of it. When the wind was calm, when it was late at night, you could hear a pin drop. I chose to find it peaceful. But this winter, the winter of 2015, had other plans.

***

IT TAKES

I can't remember when it really first started. Like a lot of "ghost stories", it began with a whisper. Little oddities, forgotten almost as soon as they occurred because they didn't merit additional thought. I had more pressing concerns.

Work, bills, food, fixing the pipes, fixing my brakes, keeping Sammy away from sharp objects, and generally surviving the brutal Canadian winter—that, and the hundred other things on my plate were more than enough to keep my mind occupied. If a door was closed when it should have been opened, I paid it no mind, I simply opened the door. If a door was unlocked when it should have been locked, I blamed the kids, and I simply locked the door.

That doesn't mean I didn't notice things though. That doesn't mean there weren't a few nights when something stuck.

***

Monday.

I didn't know what time it was. Close to midnight, maybe past. I hadn't checked, and I figured if I did check, I'd just get frustrated and then sleep would be even harder.

I hated the nights when my brain wouldn't turn off. They were infrequent, but annoying enough that I probably should have done something about it. But it was another one of those things that always got lost in the shuffle.

A.W. SCHOFIELD

After god knows how long, I stopped forcing my eyes closed and just looked into the blackness. Hoping that the lack of anything to see would convince my brain to drift far enough away that I could fall asleep.

My bedroom was the last door on the left of the long hallway; and at the very end of that hallway, there was a window.

Not much to see outside, the same view of the driveway that the living room window gave, only partially obscured by overgrown foliage. However, at night, as I lay in bed, it provided the only thing to look at as it took in the faintest glimmer of pale blue moonbeams.

Those soft, diagonal lines of displaced light carved out the silhouette of my doorframe. A tall rectangle of blue in the sea of black. It was hard not to focus on it.

But then I drifted.

I can recall a million times, these little embarrassments. It doesn't only happen when you're tired.

I used to take the bus to work, way back in the day. Back when I lived in the city.

No one wants to be on a bus. No one enjoys the bus experience. Especially not the same route twice a day every day. So what do you do? You let your brain fly away. You go somewhere else.

I became a master at this.

The only problem is that while your brain drifts away, your body doesn't. Your eyes don't.

I could be looking right at something and have no idea what I was looking at or for how long I had been looking at it.

IT TAKES

Or, in the case of a bus full of people, someone.

Those little awkward moments when you realize you've absent-mindedly been staring at someone for a length of time you cannot recall. Only noticing that you're doing it when you notice them notice you.

Then you snap. You come back online. You shake the mouse and turn off low-power mode. Falling back into yourself like falling back into your seat on the sofa.

It's a funny thing, how brains work like that.

Because I was looking at that tall blue rectangle that was my doorframe, but I wasn't seeing it. I was elsewhere, floating in the clouds for what could have been minutes or hours. Then...

Snap.

The figure in the rectangle ran away.

The figure... the silhouette of a small boy cut out of the blue. The figure I had been looking at but wasn't seeing. How long was he there?

By the time I fell back into myself, I wasn't convinced that I had seen him at all.

Sammy, I figured. I wouldn't put it past him, little kids do weird shit all the time.

I creaked out of bed and tiptoed through the threshold into the hallway. I never worried about waking Sammy up, but something in my mind decided I should be quiet anyway. Carefully I stepped towards Sammy's bedroom door, and peered inside.

Dead asleep.

Maybe I didn't see anything after all. At least, that's what I told myself. I filed it away. Paid it no mind. Just a silly little thing. But... I remembered it.

***

Wednesday.

"Dad, do you want me to be a flashlight or do you want me to Google? Pick one." Maddy hazed.

"Can't you do both?"

She scoffed and began typing awkwardly on her phone with her right hand while holding the flashlight steady with her left.

"Get under. Kneel down and shine it up."

Maddy obliged, "What the hell am I Googling?"

"Google how to fix a sink."

"I need you to be a little more specific."

"How to fix a KITCHEN sink!"

"But what part!? What are you stuck on?"

"I don't know! I'm not a plumber!"

"So call a plumber!"

"Maddy..."

"Okay, okay, fine. I'll... look up a video of someone fixing a sink and I'll tell you what they do."

"Don't worry, freak. We'll get this done quick and you can go back to your caves."

IT TAKES

Four hours later I collapsed on my bed. Letting out a deep sigh, as the subtle aches from laying awkwardly under a sink for ages rose to the surface.

The deep sigh was followed by a frustrated grumble. So many other things I had to do. Pushed another day forward.

But I took solace in finally being in bed. I fell asleep quickly. Only to wake up in the dark. Again staring out at my rectangle.

This time it was my own fault. I got too caught up, and I forgot to go to the bathroom before bed.

I removed the covers and waddled my way out the door and down the hall, quickly moving from subtle moonlight to pitch black.

Six steps forward, turn left, reach out. Sure enough, there was the bathroom door.

The sickly yellow light blinded as I flicked it on, shutting the door behind me. I always meant to get a night light for this reason. Another for the list of things I can only seem to remember when I can't do anything about it.

I did my business. My eyes crept open, slowly adjusting to the light, which would only make the dark that much darker after.

I moved to the sink and began washing my hands. The faucet gurgled at me like a dying animal before succumbing to the function it was designed for.

But, above the hiss and slight sputter of the running water, I heard another sound. Higher. Right in front of me.

Something scraping; a subtle little scratch.

My eyes flicked up toward the mirror on the face of the medicine cabinet. But as they did, they caught something falling down.

It was in my vision for only a split second, but it was instantly recognizable. A small, jagged, shard of mirror.

It glid past my eyes and fell into the basin with a sharp clink. But, as I looked down to see where it landed, it was gone.

I supposed it could've gone down the drain really fast. That would make sense enough. Then I looked into the mirror to see the damage.

Only there was none.

The mirror on the medicine cabinet, while smudged and far from pristine, was completely intact. Not a crack. Certainly no shard missing.

Strange. Maybe I didn't see anything after all. At least, that's what I told myself. I filed it away. Paid it no mind. Just another silly little thing. But... I remembered it.

I didn't think there was a ghost, or a specter, or a demon, or anything like that.

It was a trick of the shadows. It was my exhaustion. It was nothing. I had lived in this house for 17 years and nothing had ever happened, why would there be a "haunting" now? How can a house just suddenly *become* haunted?

Then there was Friday.

Then there was the basement.

IT TAKES

CHAPTER III

THE BASEMENT

I got home from work at around 7. It was deep into the cold months so it was well after dark – and 'dark' outside in Nova Scotia was DARK. No light pollution, no bustling night life, barely even street lamps. You couldn't even see the trees in the woods, it was just black on black. You could see the stars though, that's why we moved here all those years ago.

The cold was ruthlessly brisk against my face. The snow was beginning to pile up and I was praying that it would stop. So many exhausting hours wasted shovelling this damn driveway already, I didn't want to go through it again so soon.

I futzed with my keys in the dark and opened the door, happy to feel the moderate warmth. After that time our heater broke two winters ago, I still got a little nervous every now and then. Safe for the moment, though. I could also smell the cold pizza Maddy ordered. That was usually the scene. Maddy cooks sometimes, and I cook on weekends, but for the most part I just give her some money and she orders whatever for the two of them and I eat what's left.

"Right side has mushrooms." Maddy's voice called out from her room down the hall.

"Gross." I replied.

I walked over to the kitchen and opened the box to grab a fungus-less slice, but then I heard her call out again.

"Oh—by the way, what did you do to the basement door?"

Immediately my face scrunched in confusion.

"What do you mean?" I closed the box and walked into the hallway towards Maddy's room. Maddy was standing in her doorway.

"Did you repaint it or something?" She asked.

I scrunched my brow again, "Why the hell would I repaint a door?"

"Well…" Maddy responded then led me further down the hall to the basement door. "Look at it."

I scanned the door briefly, "It looks the same."

"No it doesn't, look." She said, gesturing towards it, "It used to be all scuffed up around the knob, right? And there was that big scratch from when I let Sammy have the umbrella."

I looked to the door again and sure enough… She was right. There were no marks. It didn't look freshly painted though; in some ways it looked older. It was still worn, just worn in different ways.

"What the fuck?" I responded incredulously.

"Bad word, dad." Said Sammy, now joining the conversation and giving me a hug.

"How's it goin' Sammy?" I greeted mildly, tousling his hair, while not taking my eyes off the door.

"Good. I'm bisexual." Sammy responded.

Immediately I looked at Maddy who was snickering.

"I can explain." Maddy muttered through her laughter.

"Why? Why did you do this?" I asked, exaggerating my exhaustion.

"He heard me on the phone! He asked what it meant. I told him it's when you like guys and girls, that's it! And then he just started saying it! You know how he is!" Maddy explained.

"I'm bisexual." Sammy repeated.

"Sammy you're not bisexual." I stated, wearily.

"Yes I am!"

"I mean he might be." Maddy interjected.

"He's five."

"Everyone's journey is different." Maddy said, still snickering.

I rubbed my temples and let out a deep sigh "Okay buddy, you're bisexual. Just don't say it at school, okay? I don't want more phone calls... Maddy, what the hell happened to the door?"

"I don't know, I was asking you!"

IT TAKES

"Did you open it?" I asked, seeing that as the next logical course of action.

"No, not yet."

I then gingerly grasped the doorknob and began to turn it.

It instantly felt different... Every door has a unique feeling to it. A specific smoothness and level of resistance when you turn the knob and pull it open. This door used to be snug, it used to take a bit of force but now... it was buttery smooth.

"...This is a completely different door." I said in disbelief. "No one came over or anything today, right?"

"It could've been while we were at school?" Maddy hypothesized.

"Why would someone break into our house and replace one door–it's just this door right?"

"Yeah, I think so." Maddy answered.

"Someone broke in?" Asked Sammy. I almost forgot he was listening.

"No, no, of course not." I said, only to quell his fears. I stood pondering for a minute before I continued. "I'm gonna go down there and see if there's anything weird."

"I'll come!" Sammy offered enthusiastically.

"No Sammy, stay up here with your sister." I answered. As I looked over, I noticed Maddy was already holding his arm so he didn't run ahead as I opened the door.

I looked back and I was met with the pitch black abyss. I could only see about three steps down before they were engulfed. Unfortunately, the only light switch was at the bottom, but I knew these stairs well enough.

I made my way down, unsure of what I expected to find. The stairs creaked and I was faced with the utter blackness. I almost lost my balance on the last step as I subconsciously miscounted the number of stairs, but I recovered.

I blindly reached for the light switch on the right wall. I missed at first, I figured my muscle memory was thrown off, but I reached a little bit further and found them.

I flicked the switch up and… nothing. Still pitch black. I flicked it up and down a few more times.

No luck.

"Light's not working." I called up. "Grab the flashlight for me?"

I heard two sets of footsteps walk away. Suddenly I felt a bit of unease creeping in. I couldn't put my finger on it though. Something just felt off. Like for whatever reason, I just wasn't supposed to be here.

I could only compare it to being at a party where you didn't know anybody. Your guard goes up, your mind plans an exit strategy. Except where there would be noise and laughter and chaos, there was nothing.

The cold began to give me goosebumps, the basement never heated well. And the smell… It was worse than usual. Hollow and musky like dead water or mould.

"Got it!" Maddy called down, startling me out of my weird headspace.

"Toss it down." I said, turning and cupping my hands.

IT TAKES

I could just barely see the silhouette of the flashlight coming down against the faint upstairs light, but I was able to catch it.

I turned back to the curtain of blackness and clicked on the button. The beam shot out and I gasped. Louder than I was expecting to.

"What is it!?" Maddy called down, clearly noticing the alarm in my voice.

"What the f—" I stopped myself, less because I was concerned about swearing and more because my voice was taken away.

"All our shit's gone!" I eventually exclaimed. I moved the flashlight all around and, sure enough, the basement was completely empty. All those years of clutter were gone, it was just bare wooden studs and insulation all around. The floor, a completely barren concrete slab. Nothing was left.

"What do you mean?" Maddy asked. I started to hear footsteps creaking down the stairs. I turned and ushered them back upstairs along with myself.

"Don't come down here right now. I'm gonna… I'm calling 911." I said, trying to remain calm as I reached the top of the stairs and closed the door behind me.

"What happened? Are we gonna die?" Sammy asked.

"What? No. Jesus Christ, Sammy. We're fine. Just… chill. Maddy, take him and go to your room."

"Okay, but what do you mean it's all gone? That doesn't make sense." Maddy asked incredulously.

I struggled to explain it any better, "It's all gone. Literally all of it. I don't know. Someone just... I don't know."

Maddy continued, attempting to force logic into it, "Someone... took all our old junk? Didn't feel like taking the TV or the computers or anything?"

"Yeah? Maybe? I don't know what to tell you, I guess they were pretty stupid. Still though, just stay in your room for now. Double check nothing else was taken and... don't teach Sammy any new words, please."

"Uh, Sure... Alright Sammy, let's go play in my room. We can explore your identity further." Maddy said as she walked him away.

I tried to keep things light and not let on the gravity of the situation. I didn't want them to worry or panic. I wanted to manage this as much as I could. If I could make the kids believe it was just some idiot and they had nothing to worry about, that's what I would do.

But I didn't think that was the case. Sure, what they did was peculiar, but they still got in and out without a trace. They knew when we wouldn't be home. They covered their tracks. There was a method to this.

I called the police. I knew there wasn't much they could do. I honestly didn't care about recovering all our stuff. Like Maddy said, it was all junk. 90% of it wouldn't be missed. I just needed them to make sure we were safe.

While I waited for someone to arrive, I checked all the windows and doors. We're a small, single floor house, so there's not that many points of entry. Everything was locked up as it should be. I also managed to squeeze in a slice of cold pizza while I looked.

There was a spare key under a rock on the walkway for the kids since I'm not always around, that was the only explanation I could think of. If this person was watching us, then they might have seen the kids use it… That thought deeply unsettled me.

A single officer showed up at the door. Predictably, he didn't give much in the way of answers or solutions. He seemed as perplexed as I did. He checked out the basement a little bit, checked the windows and doors, took a little walk around the perimeter, then said to call if anything else happened.

That was about what I expected, but it put my mind a little at ease that he didn't turn up anything alarming. He said the house seemed to be secure. So I figured I just wouldn't do the spare key thing anymore.

He left, and I went back to check in on the kids. Sammy was asleep in Maddy's bed while Maddy was sitting up next to him scrolling on her phone. It made me both proud and sad to see Maddy be so good with her brother like that. She was truly a great kid. She always stepped up. I just wish she didn't always have to.

"He's out, huh?" I said quietly.

"Yup. I used his dragon book. Always works." Maddy replied.

"Alright I'll get him outta your hair." I said, walking over and picking up his limp 40 pound frame.

"So what happened? What are they gonna do?" She asked.

"Uh. Nothing… But hey, if anything this guy did us a favor—clearing that basement out."

"I bet it was mom, coming back to get an old dress for a date or something. Then covering her tracks by taking everything else." She barbed.

I laughed, "That would be interesting. I heard she was in Hawaii though, with her second family."

"Really? I thought it was Cancun."

"No, that's her third family."

"Wow, how many families does she have again?"

"I don't know but she is VERY happy. She sends me voicemails specifically telling me how much she loves all her other kids more than you." I quipped, making sure the sarcasm was more than apparent just to be safe.

"Oh good for her!"

"I know right? You love to see it. You love to see people thrive." I joked as I walked out with Sammy.

The deadbeat mom jokes started when Maddy turned 15. She made a crack about her mother being too busy to show because of some wild scenario she conjured up.

Sometimes she joined the circus, sometimes she was a super spy in a top secret undercover mission, and sometimes she had a bunch of better, richer, and cooler families.

I acknowledge that this was maybe not the healthiest coping mechanism to indulge with a child whose mother left her—I resisted and scolded for a while, but sometimes you just have to make fun where you can. There's only so much you can let it hurt, and it hurt for a long time.

In reality, she wasn't a bad person. We both knew that, deep down. It was just easier to pretend that she was, and make a game of it.

"Are we safe though?" Maddy asked, with a seriousness returning to her tone.

"Yeah. We're safe. We're locked up tight. I got rid of the spare key just in case… We're good. I imagine they got whatever they were looking for anyway." I still tried my best to sound convincingly nonchalant.

I put Sammy to bed, not bothering to be super delicate. That kid could sleep through Armageddon. Then I went to bed myself, indulging my ritual of watching an hour or two of TV on the old 90s box at my bedside before passing out.

I always liked the classic tube TVs, so when we finally upgraded our living room one to a slim fella, I kept the old one for me. The glow, the hum, and the muffled audio were oddly soothing.

The TV provided a decent distraction for a while, caught some late night talk shows. Wasn't the same since Craig Ferguson retired but it was usually good enough.

I couldn't help thinking about all the weirdness of today, though. Nevermind the past week. I could deny it to the kids, but I couldn't deny it to myself that I was spooked. Every now and then I'd mute the TV, thinking I heard something that was clearly just the house settling. Take a glance out my doorway to see if anything was there.

I just had this feeling deep in my gut that something was very wrong, and that this wasn't over…

Sleep didn't come easy that night, I habitually checked on the kids at least half a dozen times and quadruple checked the locks. Eventually I allowed myself to calm down and drift off to sleep.

I wish it lasted. Unfortunately, the night wasn't done with me.

I woke up around 3 a.m. to the sound of a distant phone ringing. Not my cellphone, not Maddy's, but our landline out in the living room.

Indeed, we still had a landline. Cell reception out here was spotty sometimes so it helped, but it very rarely got use anymore. I can't remember the last time I heard it ring. I don't even know how many people still had the number. Let alone who would have the number that would call this late at night.

I hesitantly climbed out of bed, made my way through the hall, and into the living room. The more open space and plentiful windows allowed more of that blue moonlight glow. I walked over and picked up the ringing phone. As I put it to my ear, I was instantly overcome by loud sounds of audio distortion and crackling. I held the phone an extra inch or two away from my ear.

"Hello?" I asked quietly, "Who is this?"

There was no immediate response amidst the noise, so after a few seconds I gave it one more, louder attempt.

"Hello?"

IT TAKES

After about 20 more seconds of dead air, an old and sickly voice finally came through.

"I remember." It croaked.

The call cut off. I stood there in the dark, petrified, listening to the dial tone.

What the hell did that mean? Was that a threat? Was this the person who robbed us? I thought maybe it was at first, but when I really analyzed the voice... it didn't seem right.

They sounded bad. Really bad. And the way they said it... it wasn't threatening. It didn't even sound like they were talking to me.

I had no idea what to make of it. I chalked it up to a wrong number... but the timing of it was just... too freaky.

I had an even harder time getting back to sleep after that. It was a race to fall asleep before the sun rose. I just barely was able to.

CHAPTER IV
THE UNFAMILIAR

Most Saturdays would begin with Sammy waking me up unceremoniously at around 6 or 7 am for one thing or another.

These days he at least whispered instead of screaming and jumping on my chest. Progress.

This morning though, no Sammy. I woke up by myself around 8:30. I couldn't help but feel relieved. It's exceptionally rare that my sleep gets to end naturally, so I decided to savor it… Until a thought crept into my head.

Everything from the night before was lagging behind my consciousness, but it all came back to me in a rush.

Sammy didn't always wake me up, but for him to not wake me up today… I had to go check on him.

I rushed out of bed and down the hallway. I peeked into Maddy's room. She was there. Good. One sigh of relief. Then I reached Sammy's room and…

IT TAKES

Gone.

I felt the urge to panic rising—those pins and needles that precede the rush of every possible bad thing that could have happened—but I talked myself down. He could be up playing in the living room or something.

I darted to the living room, but still no Sammy.

I moved to the bathroom. No Sammy. I went to the kitchen. I double checked Maddy's room. I double checked my room. I looked in the front yard. The back yard. The damn linen closet… Nothing.

My heart raced. I couldn't breathe. Fear and guilt swirled like a hurricane in my head. Why did I let him sleep alone after all this? Why didn't I keep watch all night? No, this couldn't be happening…

Then it hit me. One place I forgot to check.

The basement.

A chill ran down my spine as I thought of it. But why? Why would this thought fill me with dread? It was just our basement. I couldn't understand it.

I walked to the basement door, gazing at its subtle unfamiliarities.

I reached out. The knob turned easy and the door gave no resistance, like it was begging to be opened.

This time, the basement wasn't a pitch-black void. The early morning sun shone its light through the small window on the far end and generously illuminated the space I was descending into.

I could see all the stairs now and yet even so, I still tripped at the end. Nearly falling on my face. Odd, but my adrenaline was high. I didn't dwell.

In the middle of the grey concrete, I saw my boy lying there on his side in his jammies. I exhaled. I was so relieved, I wanted to rush over and squeeze the life out of him, but I resisted the impulse and instead gently lifted his face off the cold floor. He began to stir as I did.

"Dad?" He muttered weakly.

I breathed one more sigh of relief. "Holy shit Sammy, you scared me to death. What are you doing here?"

"Bad word." He responded.

"I know. I'm working on it, I really am."

"Where am I?"

"You're... In the basement, buddy. You don't remember coming down here?"

"No... But I was dreaming about it I think..."

That answer sent a slight shiver. Especially since Sammy had never sleepwalked before.

"God you're a weird kid. Okay let's get you out of here, it's freezing. You could have frozen your damn face off on his concrete."

I hoisted Sammy up and put him on my back as I started to walk out... But I stopped as I began to really take in my surroundings. This was the first time I could actually see the basement in decent enough light since the incident and it was... wrong.

It wasn't just all of our missing items making the space feel open and uncanny, like when you move your furniture and the whole room suddenly looks bigger... No, there was something else.

IT TAKES

The stairs... I didn't miscount them. There were one too many. The light switch really was a few inches further from the corner than it should be.

Not only that—the wooden beams across the ceiling, the studs across the walls, they were spaced just a little too far apart. The insulation, the pipes, the wiring, it all looked off. Even the ceiling hung ever so slightly higher.

It wasn't just the door that was different now... Everything was different.

This... was not our basement.

CHAPTER V

TICK TOCK

I couldn't believe my eyes. This had to be some kind of mistake—some kind of trick. I quickly brought Sammy upstairs. My first instinct was to get him out of this place, but then I headed back down. How could I not? I had to make sense of this.

I stared into the uncanny open room. I tried to fit the square peg of what my eyes were giving me into the round hole of my memory but it would not fit. Did it just look different because it was empty?

No. This wasn't just some half-remembered temporary space that could change without me knowing, this was 17 years of my life. It was not the same room. But how?

I looked at it from every rational angle that I could try to find, desperate for something to cling to. To remove all of our belongings and perform a complete structural

IT TAKES

renovation, this would have had to be done over weeks. There was about a 6 hour window every weekday where no one was home.

They would have had to bring trucks, hire contractors, then do a complete clean and leave no trace, no smell, no anything, before 3 pm—and I guess just hope that nobody came home early or checked the basement before it was done.

Even assuming that it would be possible to do this—which it wouldn't be—why?

Why replace a room with another room that looks almost identical but not quite? If they were really trying to make it look like the same room, they could have tried harder.

With the amount of dedication it would take to complete this project, surely they would know to get the number of stairs right. They didn't seem concerned with convincing me it's the same room, so what was the point?

And also... what was that sound? I thought I heard it the first night when I came down, but I was too shocked to really process it. What was it?

It was some kind of ticking. Very faint, almost inaudible, but the basement was so deathly quiet otherwise that I couldn't help but fixate on it. I listened harder.

Tick tock. Tick tock.

A clock... Definitely a clock... But there was no clock in here. I scoured the place again just to be sure. Nothing; and the sound never seemed to get closer no matter where I moved in the space. What was making this damn sound and where was it coming from?

It was driving me insane. All of it. Every single aspect of this impossible room. They always say the most logical explanation is usually the right one, but this had no logical explanations. The closest thing to a logical explanation was that I was losing my mind.

I had to look harder. There had to be something here that could tell me more.

As I scanned the walls, I saw something that might have answers–tucked away in the back, obscured by the stairs: the breaker box.

That had to tell me something. Would it still work? Would it still be all wired in? Would the labels I scribbled next to the switches still be there? I walked over and prepared to open the door.

"Dad?" Maddy's voice called out, startling me.

"Maddy! Shit, you scared me. What are you doing up so early?"

"Sammy woke me up."

I looked over and saw both of them standing in the middle of the concrete floor. I didn't like seeing them in this place. It felt dangerous. Foreign. Unknown.

Maddy continued as she took a look around the somewhat lit room, "What... What's going on?"

I began ushering the two of them up the rickety stairs. "It's okay. Everything's fine. Let's just stay out of here for now, alright?"

I got the three of us out and shut the door behind me, trying to shake the weirdness from my head.

"I'm hungry." Sammy piped up.

IT TAKES

Before I could answer, Maddy stepped in "Go sit at the table, bud. We'll grab you something in a second." I could instantly read her intentions. She saw it too.

"Yeah, how about I make us all pancakes, huh?" I offered. "Its been awhile, hasn't it?"

"Yes! Its been forever!" Sammy said dramatically before running off with a huge grin.

Maddy turned to me, her expression filled with worry, "What the hell was that?" she uttered under her breath.

"Maddy, I really don't know." My instincts told me to play dumb and not scare her, but I knew I couldn't.

"But you saw it right? I mean obviously you noticed."

Reluctantly I had to admit it. "Yeah, I noticed."

"How is that possible? How did that happen?" Her voice now filled with tension and unease.

"I told you, I don't know." I answered as calmly as possible.

"W... What the hell do we do?"

"I'm working on it. I'll figure it out. We'll be fine. Until then, we're just not gonna go down there anymore. I'll get a lock so Dummy doesn't sleepwalk down there again."

"Sammy sleepwalked? Sammy doesn't sleepwalk, dad."

"Maddy, we will be fine. I promise." I asserted.

I hated lying to them. I wanted to be that dad that never lied and always told it like it is, but I just couldn't bear having them as worried and scared as I was. So I had to employ the dad bravado. Put the bass in the voice. Exude confidence. The "you're safe with me because dad can handle anything" gimmick.

I got pretty good at putting that on over the years. I had to, it was a necessity. But it always felt like cosplay. Pretending the be the dad I wished I was. The fear I felt today was just another, stranger version of the fear I've felt a thousand times.

I never knew what I was doing. I never knew how to raise them. I was unqualified and in over my head from day one. This though, this was another level of unqualified.

***

The rest of the day went by as normally as it could. We had a movie night. It was a good way to keep the kids close to me for a while.

Sammy was his usual self. Maddy didn't bring up the subject again, though I could see it in her eyes. Eventually they went off to bed, but not me.

I waited until I knew they were asleep, then I grabbed the flashlight and headed downstairs again. Back into the dark. My instincts told me not to go down there again, but I had to see the breaker.

I readied myself for the extra step and made it down safely. The basement looked horrifying to me now, especially in the dark. This space that shouldn't be empty. This space that's so familiar but ever so slightly wrong. Sitting below us every moment.

I began to wonder how long it had been since I was in the basement before all this. How long could it have been like this and gone unnoticed? Days? Weeks? I shuddered.

IT TAKES

Tick Tock. Tick Tock. That maddening sound remained. The sound with no discernable origin, amidst the complete silence.

That was another thing that bothered me, but I didn't know why until this moment.

It shouldn't be silent. I should hear the low hum of the boiler. I should hear the rattling of the pipes as hot air gets pumped through.

But I didn't.

It was dead down here. That was the word that kept flashing in my mind over and over. It's dead.

But if it was so dead, then why didn't I feel alone?

I hurried over to the breaker box. It looked about the same on the outside. Big grey panel with a door. Promising, but I didn't imagine they came in too many variants. Then I opened it and shone the flashlight inside. My stomach sank.

It was wrong. The switches were wrong. The labels by the switches were wrong. Still handwritten, but not MY handwriting. I looked at the labels themselves. "Bath 2" "Dining" "Attic"–we didn't have those rooms. This made even less sense.

I stared at the labels, trying to somehow decipher some kind of meaning, some kind of intent.

Then... the gentlest little movement in the air hit the back of my neck. So subtle that I may not have paid it any mind, except for the fact that it was warm.

I gasped. Goosebumps instantly formed all through my body and I spun around violently, pointing the flashlight to face the origin of that sensation. All that the flashlight illuminated was the empty room.

I didn't know what to believe. I didn't know what I thought that was. All I knew was that I did not want to be here anymore. Not for one more second.

So I made a break for it. I scurried upstairs, shutting the door, and attempted to shake off the fear. I propped an extra chair from the kitchen table in front of the door. Mostly so that Sammy couldn't get down there again; but also, admittedly, because I was terrified.

IT TAKES

CHAPTER VI

THE CHILD

I was at a loss. My brain was filled with questions, but I felt powerless to do anything about it. What could I do? How could I get answers?

I walked hastily down the hall to my bedroom. I sat in bed and hopped on my laptop to try a few internet searches, but to no avail.

Nobody else seemed to have had an experience like this before, or at least they hadn't posted about it anywhere that I could see. Though I wasn't the most adept at internet stuff.

But then a sound broke my concentration. A familiar sound.

The landline was ringing again. I felt a sense of dread course through me. This couldn't be a coincidence, and I didn't want to hear that voice again. But I had to answer.

IT TAKES

I walked back out of my room, through the hallway, awkwardly sidling past the chair against that damn basement door, and into the living room once again.

I could barely see anything, my eyes had yet to adjust to the dark, but I could maneuver well enough. I made it to the phone and picked it up.

"Hello?" I spoke, hesitantly. I was immediately confronted with thick static again. No semblance of a voice within it.

"Hello?" I repeated. I waited about a solid minute listening to the static before deciding to give up. Then it happened.

Just as I pulled the phone away from my ear, I heard a fraction of a voice. The slightest hint of vocalization. I couldn't make it out, but it didn't sound like the same one as before. I put the phone back to my ear.

"Who is this?" I asked, waiting another few seconds.

"Daddy?" A childlike voice spoke from the other end and a chill ran through my entire body like a shockwave. It was muffled, barely audible through the static, but I could tell it was a young voice.

"Who is this?" I asked again, trying to enunciate more.

"Daddy?" They repeated with the same inflection and intonation. They sounded a bit surprised, like they weren't expecting to talk to me.

"I—I think you have the wrong number. Are you... Okay? Do you need help?"

"Daddy?" Again. The exact same. Like it was a playback on loop. Then the call dropped.

I stood there holding the receiver in my hand, unable to move. What the hell was that? Any other time, I might have thought that was a random wrong number, but with everything happening... It couldn't have been.

My mind spun. Who was that kid? They sounded about Sammy's age. It almost sounded like it WAS Sammy, but Sammy doesn't call me "daddy."

Now creeped out and confused beyond my wits, I could only just compulsively check the door locks and windows again. It felt like the only tangible thing I could do. The only slim bit of control I had over anything.

Doors locked. Windows locked. I looked out each window, not sure what I was expecting to see. Hopefully nothing, though, it was easy to see nothing since it was basically just pitch black dotted with falling snow.

The only outside light being in the front yard. the faint glow of a somewhat nearby streetlight cascading in through the gap in the wall of trees where the long, gravel driveway starts.

As I looked out the living room window, I knew the view I expected. I knew that subtle fuzz of soft light. How it would be partially broken by the silhouette of my car in the driveway. That was the view I expected. It wasn't the view I got.

Sure, it was mostly the same. But there was a second silhouette blotting out the light. Right near the entrance of the driveway. A figure, just standing there.

I almost jumped out of my skin. I was already on edge, but this nearly sent me over the top. We were supposed to be next to nowhere. There was no good reason for a person to be standing there in the middle of the night. I contained myself just enough to put the figure into focus and see what it was.

It was small. Maybe three or four feet tall, it was difficult to tell from the distance... A child?

I squinted harder and got confirmation. It looked like a little boy. I began to panic. Was it Sammy? The silhouette didn't look exactly like him but... I had to check. I sprinted through the living room, through the narrow hallway, and burst into Sammy's room to see if he was still in bed.

He was gone. My heart sank. That figure must have been him. He must have been sleepwalking again.

I ran back out, through the hallway, through the living room, and through the front door, not bothering to grab my coat or my boots, which was a mistake. I barreled down the driveway, the few inches of snow on the ground providing little comfort against the sharp, jagged gravel.

I winced in pain and shuddered as the unforgiving cold pierced my body, but when I reached the end, I saw no one. The figure was gone. I looked down both sides of the road and couldn't see a soul.

"Sammy!" I yelled out in either direction, to no response as puffs of ghostly steam floated from my mouth. I wanted to run out and look further but without any light, it would be hopeless. I needed my car.

I sprinted back into the house and grabbed the keys, but stopped as critical thought began to flow into my panicked mind...

I didn't want to have to bring Maddy into this, but I had no choice. I had to wake her up and get her to keep watch in case he came back.

I ran through the living room and down the hallway to Maddy's room... but once again my brain stopped me before opening her door.

Once again I looked, without seeing. I had missed what was right in front of me.

This time not from daydreaming or fatigue, but from chaos. I missed it. Something so obvious.

I had run down the hallway when I was checking if Sammy was there, and I ran down it again now... unimpeded. The chair I propped up in front of the basement door was gone.

I knew where Sammy was. He wasn't outside at all. He was down there. I didn't hesitate. I opened the door and descended the stairs, flashlight be damned.

"Sammy?" I called out into the opaque blackness.

I slowly stepped across the concrete, careful not to bump into Sammy if he was indeed here. My eyes didn't adjust to the dark at all.

I knelt down, feeling around, hoping to find Sammy asleep like he was before, but my hand wasn't catching anything, and it was so, so cold.

"Sam!" I yelled into the blanket of darkness.

"Daddy?" A deathly soft, childlike voice called out from behind me. I jumped and spun around to face it, despite not being able to see a thing.

It wasn't Sammy. Was it? It didn't sound right. But it sounded close.

IT TAKES

"Dad?" Another soft voice called out, from almost the same direction. Just a little bit to the left. So similar to the other one, but ever so slightly more distinct and clear. THIS was Sammy's voice. It had to be. But what the hell was the other one? It sounded... exactly like the voice from the phone.

I hurried cautiously in his direction, and eventually my hands found him. I grabbed him and pulled him into a hug.

"Oh, Sammy. There you are." I exclaimed, relieved. "Buddy, what are we gonna do about this sleepwalking?"

Sammy didn't hug me back, he just stood there in silence for a moment. I heard his soft breathing. For a split second a terrifying thought entered my mind. But it washed away when he finally responded.

"I wasn't sleepwalking." he mumbled.

I was confused, but I scooped Sammy up and rushed him upstairs before I questioned him further, closing the door tight behind us.

I caught my breath for a second, then knelt down to look at him. He looked dazed, and pale.

"You weren't sleepwalking?" I asked.

"No." Sammy responded wearily.

"Then why did you go down there? I told you not to go down there anymore."

"I'm sorry, dad... The man made me go there." He explained, his tone of voice never changing.

"The... man?" My blood went cold and my breath got caught in my throat, "What man? Who are you talking about?"

"The scary man... from my dream... The Sharp Man."

A.W. SCHOFIELD

IT TAKES

CHAPTER VII
SIGHT UNSEEN

I lost my words for a minute. I didn't know how to respond to that. What did 'The Sharp Man' mean?

"So... You WERE dreaming then?" I questioned.

"No. He's for real. He's one of them. He's down there." Sammy continued to murmur.

I thought about the other voice in the basement... the voice on the phone... the figure outside.

"Is he a boy? Is he little?" I asked.

"No, he's tall like you. But he's very scary, I don't like him. I don't like how he smiles."

How he smiles? That made me shiver. I tried not to let it show.

"Okay." I accepted. "Why is he sharp?"

"That's what we call it." Sammy answered, cryptically.

"That's what you call what? Who's we?"

IT TAKES

Sammy just shrugged his shoulders and let out a deep yawn. The kid looked barely awake so I stopped my line of questioning for now and put him to bed. Didn't want to risk freaking him out too much.

I took inventory of what I knew as I sat awake in bed, the static from the old TV hissing at me.

The basement was not my basement. There was a "Sharp Man." There was a child. There was the other sickly voice on the phone. There was even that shard of the bathroom mirror that broke off but then didn't. What did it all mean? How did it connect? More importantly, what could I do? How could I keep us safe?

Should I leave? I thought. Should I take the kids and run? It was tempting, but where could we go? I couldn't afford another house. Shit, I couldn't even afford an apartment these days. Wherever we went, whichever crummy motel, we would eventually have to come back.

No, there had to be a way to fix this... I just needed help.

The biggest hurdle I had to overcome was accepting that there were forces at work beyond my understanding. I'm an atheist. I believe in science; I believe in what can be proven. I've lived that way for my entire life and I'd never had it disputed until now. But I was getting nowhere expecting a rational explanation to pop up out of thin air, so I had to remove that from the equation.

Once I acknowledged that I could not understand these things, the clearest option became to find someone who could.

Lynn Barnes. Parapsychologist & psychic medium. I found her on Facebook. Her page looked promising and she seemed nice. I scheduled her to come over the following afternoon.

***

I didn't get much sleep that night. I spent the early hours of the morning tidying up, it had been a hot minute since we had a guest.

Sammy awoke, not seeming to sweat any of what happened the previous night. Maddy crawled out of bed a few hours later.

"Whoa, you cleaned?" She said in a groggy voice as she wiped the sleep from her eyes.

"Yeah, we're gonna have someone coming over in... well any minute now probably."

"Oh. Who?"

The words formed in my brain but got stopped by the bouncer before they could exit my mouth. It sounded stupid. I tried to find another way to say it, but I was unsuccessful.

"A psychic." I said, trying to sound assured in my decision.

Immediately Maddy let out a chuckle. "THAT'S what we're doing?"

IT TAKES

"Hey, listen, it couldn't hurt to get another perspective, alright?" I explained.

"But a psychic!?" She pushed, "Dad, that stuff isn't real!"

"Yeah, well, neither is any of this! Let's just give her a chance. See what she has to say."

Maddy sighed. "I'm gonna ask you a question, and I need you to be honest with me."

"What's your question, Maddy?"

"Did you find them on Facebook?"

I shot her a glare. "Okay, see this is why I don't bring you into the decision-making process. You're just all judgment."

"Dad, what the hell?"

"We're giving her a chance. We're being open-minded. Okay? Then if you have a suggestion, I will be open-minded to your suggestion." I said in full dad voice.

She shook her head and rolled her eyes all at once. Admittedly it seemed like a good idea at 2 a.m., and maybe less so now, but I had to commit.

A car rolled down the driveway right on cue. Out stepped a middle-aged woman with greying curly hair wearing a loud, patterned dress; along with a younger, well dressed blond man.

They rang the bell and I opened the door for them with a smile, inviting them inside.

I asked them about the drive up and all the usual nice things you're supposed to say before you actually start talking. Maddy stood there silently with a facetious grin. Eventually we all got seated in the living room.

"I know I got here a little early, I hope you don't mind." Lynn said. She had a very kind and disarming voice, "It's just that I could sense some urgency when we talked so I wanted to get here right away–and you never know with the weather these days."

"Oh, no, that's perfect. Thank you for coming... I don't know exactly where to... I mean... I never really believed in this stuff, you know?"

Lynn chuckled, "Oh don't worry, I get that all the time. I know it's a lot to try and understand."

"It is a lot, yeah. This whole thing has been... crazy."

"I bet. You said it's just you and... was it two kiddos?"

"Yeah just me and Madison here, and Sam–he's in his room."

"And the mother, is she...?"

"Gone. She's... she's gone." I said, not caring to elaborate.

Lynn nodded. "I see. That makes sense."

"That... makes sense?" I questioned.

"Well... I've been feeling it ever since I walked into this house. Sometimes these things take a little time for me to read clearly, but other times it can be just like that." Lynn snapped her fingers. "I know this may be hard for you to hear, and you're not going to want to believe it, but there is a presence here, Mr. Lewis. This is going to be difficult, but I believe the spirit of your wife still resides here."

"...Is that so." I responded flatly.

I looked over at Maddy only to see her staring daggers at me. I responded with a defeated sneer.

"Yes, but what she wants you to know—and what's important that you know, is that even though she has left this plane, she will never truly leave you."

Maddy made some kind of noise. Looking over again, her head was hanging down and her hand was covering her mouth.

So Maddy was right. I was wrong. I let the psychics finish up their whole rigmarole and they went on their way. Predictably, they made no mention of a child or a tall man or anything of the sort. As I closed the door, I didn't even have to look at Maddy to see the smug look on her face.

"Shut up." I said as I walked by.

"I just..."

"Yeah, yeah, yeah. What's your idea then? I'm all ears." I scoffed.

"Okay." Maddy began. "First off, a construction worker. Or an architect. Someone who builds or renovates houses. Get them to come in and see what they can tell us about the basement. They would probably be able to find serial numbers, model numbers, something that can be traced back to a manufacturer. There would have to be a paper trail somewhere. You just went straight to "ghosts did it"–someone had to build this. Someone had to get the materials from somewhere."

"Okay, sure, that might give us something. Good idea. I know a few contractors; I can talk to them... But I didn't just jump to ghosts, Maddy. You didn't see—" I cut myself off.

"Didn't see what?" She pushed.

I shook my head in silence. I didn't want to drag her into this any further than she already was. I felt bad enough involving her at all.

Maddy studied my lack of response before finding her words, "You can tell me shit, you know? Like, I can maybe help."

"No."

"No?" Maddy repeated, taken aback.

"Yeah, no. That's not how this is supposed to go. I know you're 17 now but... you're 17. You're my kid. This is not yours to deal with, it's mine. It's my job."

"Really?" Maddy responded with offense clearly taken. "Dad, you have always needed my help. Ever since mom left. I know you're proud or whatever but—"

"This isn't about pride, this is about you!" I snapped, "You shouldn't have to deal with these things! You are a child!"

"Yeah but I do! I do deal with them!" Her voice raised. "And it's fine that I deal with them because they need to be dealt with and you can't do it alone. That's the situation we're in. 'Shouldn't' doesn't matter, what matters is Sammy and he needs both of us."

I'd like to think that I was telling the truth when I said it wasn't about pride, but when she said I couldn't do it alone, it did hurt. It hurt because she was right. It hurt because this wasn't the first time we've had this conversation.

"Sammy is what matters, but you're both my kids. You matter too." I responded.

"Oh shut up, dad. Don't start talking like that."

IT TAKES

My eyes widened. "Did you just tell me to shut up?"

"Yes I did." A smile began to form on her face.

"...Wow." I scoffed.

"You deserved it." She added.

"Did I?"

"Yes."

"You know if I was a different kind of dad, you would not be speaking to me that way."

"Yeah, 'if'. Now just tell me what's really going on."

Maybe it was just me being a pushover, or maybe it was because I agreed with her when she said that Sammy needed both of us but... I told her. I explained the phone calls, the voices, the figures, the things Sammy was saying. I told her about The Sharp Man.

CHAPTER VIII
STATIC

I could see in her eyes that she was trying to wrap her head around it in real time. I don't know if she fully believed me, but I knew she was all-in regardless. I couldn't help but think I made another mistake by telling her.

She said she would look online for anything that might give us answers. I already tried but she was way better at navigating the online world. She could always sort the real stuff from the bullshit, I don't know how. I left her to it.

That night, I moved Sammy's bed into my room. I closed my bedroom door and hung a windcatcher from the knob so I would be able to hear if anything moved. That put my mind somewhat at ease.

The thought of going back to work in the morning didn't sit right. I couldn't wait a week to find out what's going on. I had a window while the kids were at school to figure this out, and I had to use it. Luckily I had accumulated about four sick days in almost 15 years and it was time to put them to use. I called in, and then I called a friend who does home renos to come over tomorrow. Maddy was right, that might be something.

Then it was time to try and get a good night's sleep... though I knew it was wishful thinking.

The first time I awoke was only a few hours after falling asleep. I awoke to the faint sound of the landline ringing once again.

I was tempted to go pick it up, but nothing was going to make me leave Sammy alone, not even for a second. I let it ring and eventually it stopped. Sammy was still in his bed, fast asleep. Thank god.

The second time I woke up to a different familiar sound, along with a bright flickering light illuminating the room. The glow of the TV, and the hiss of the static. I was so used to this sound. I'd accidentally fallen asleep with the TV on many times.

I sat up and first checked Sammy's bed. The lump under the blankets and the mess of brown hair sticking out of the top of them was gone. Sammy was gone. Before I could panic, however, my eyes moved to the TV and there he was. His head silhouetted in front of the monochromatic snow.

He was... just sitting and staring at it. Relief quickly turned to unease.

I creaked my way out of bed and knelt down beside him. He didn't acknowledge me in any way. Just kept staring at the screen.

"Sam. What are you doing?" I called out quietly.

"They always say the same things..." Sammy muttered, not averting his gaze.

"Who does?"

"They all do."

I was as confused as I was tired. "...What are they saying?" I asked.

Sammy pointed at the screen and just said, "Listen."

Curiosity outweighed my trepidation and I slowly leaned towards the fuzzy screen.

"It's just noise, Sammy. It's static."

"Listen." He repeated.

I focused all my attention towards the scraping hiss. I sat there trying to immerse myself enough to hear beyond the garbled mess, but nothing came through. Until...

"Daddy?" That voice. The voice from the phone. The one from the basement. It was hidden deep within the hiss, but it was there. Unmistakable. I jerked backwards in confusion and horror. Sammy kept staring. Never taking his eyes away.

Another minute or so passed. I was intent to hear more. The sound began to feel almost hypnotic. I began hearing scrambled up voices, but I couldn't tell how many of them were real and how many were just my mind playing tricks.

Words started coming through... Far away words. Like screams in a hurricane.

"No!" Yelled a desperate and horrified feminine voice.

"I don't want to." Pleaded another feminine voice.

"Why am I here?" Asked a confused, masculine voice.

IT TAKES

"The house..." Said a deeper masculine voice.

"I'm sorry..." Uttered a mournful masculine voice.

Over a dozen of these little meaningless phrases popping up through the snow, and repeating at random intervals. Maybe it was picking up some kind of signal or interference? That's what my rational brain wanted to think. But we were beyond that now.

"I remember." That old, sickly voice from the first phone call returned as well, filling me with dread.

Amongst all the odd phrases scattering through the noise, two stood out to me because they were names. 'Jacob'–yelled in a terrified manner. But even more chilling was "Caleb'–uttered through violent sobs and hysterical screams. It was ghastly.

Jacob. Caleb. Who were they? Who were any of these people? What did the words mean? Why did they repeat over and over?

My mind spun with questions as my hypnosis deepened. I could only listen and I could only stare. I listened to the words so many times. Trying to gauge their exact cadence. Trying to decipher their purpose. I think at some point I forgot to blink because the only thing that broke me from my gaze was the intense discomfort in my eyes.

I shut and rubbed them vigorously to remove the stinging. The bright 4:3 rectangle was seared into my vision. It took minutes for it to fade away.

"Sammy, stop staring at the TV. Go back to bed, okay?" I said through closed eyes.

But when my eyes opened, Sammy was no longer sitting beside me. He was back in his bed, turned towards the wall like he had been at the beginning of the night.

I looked over at my alarm clock and it read 4:02 a.m. Two hours had passed.

This couldn't be possible. Was I really transfixed for that long? Had the time really gotten away from me like that? When did Sammy go back to bed? Did... did he ever actually get up?

Fatigue overwhelmed my senses and I collapsed on my bed. When I woke up for a third time, it was finally morning. With the clarity of the sunrise and my somewhat well-rested consciousness, it seemed to me like last night was a dream.

That experience didn't feel quite as grounded as this felt now. Though I couldn't definitively say either way. It frustrated me not to know, but I still made sure to remember those names.

Martin came by early in the morning, right after I sent the kids to school. It was quite a task trying to explain to him what I needed without sounding crazy. I decided the best explanation was no explanation at all. I simply told him to look around the basement and see what he can tell me about it.

He looked around with me for about fifteen minutes. At first he seemed unsure and lackadaisical, but I noticed his brow start to furrow at certain things. He started looking more vigorously, and he'd shoot me these confused looks. Finally, he walked over and gave me his conclusion.

"Well. It looks like a basement."

"Great." I answered sarcastically.

"I mean it LOOKS like a basement. Who built this?"

"That's what I'm trying to figure out. What do you mean it 'LOOKS' like a basement?"

"I mean it is a basement, obviously, but it's not... functional. The breaker is for a completely different house. Some kind of dummy breaker, I don't know what that's about. It's wired in, but there's zero electricity going through it. The boiler is just for show, it doesn't seem to have been turned on in years. I don't know how you're getting hot water or power. The air vents are constructed fine but they don't seem to match up or make sense for the way your house is laid out and, again, they're not functional..."

"But I have electricity." I challenged. "I FEEL heat coming from the floor vents upstairs. How does that work?"

"It doesn't. It shouldn't. I mean I don't know if you're trying to fuck with me, or what's going on here but..."

I raised my hands and cut him off. "What if I told you all of this happened last week?"

"What? What do you mean 'happened'?"

"I mean my basement wasn't like this before." I explained. "The boiler worked, the breaker was fine, everything was fine. Then someone changed it... to this."

"That's... not possible, Adam. Look at the boiler, look at the pipes, look at the state of them. No one 'changed' this. It's clear as day, this has not been moved or touched in years."

"Okay. I get that... But it happened. It changed. Everything changed. It wasn't like this before... You're saying there's no way that's possible?"

"Yeah, there's no way that's possible. What's really going on here, man?"

"A lot... Look, you don't have to believe me, that's fine, I just need you to help me figure out where this stuff comes from. Are there serial numbers? Can you trace the manufacturers? Find who did the construction? Can you give me anything?"

"I... I mean, not really. I'm a contractor, I'm not the FBI. If this was a very recent job, maybe I could see about finding the records, but this was NOT a recent job. I'd guess it was remodeled in the 90s, but never finished. Originally built... who knows. I can tell you it's probably local stuff. Your insulation, these fiberglass batts, they're the ones we use a lot. This kind of boiler is common for this area and this climate. Rare to see one of these elsewhere. Seems to be the old standard model they used in the 90s and early 2000s... That's what I got for you."

I sighed with resignation. "Alright, well that's not nothing... Oh, one more thing?"

"Yeah?"

"That ticking noise... Do you have any idea what's making it?"

Martin's face scrunched in confusion again. "I just thought you had a grandfather clock upstairs or something..."

IT TAKES

Martin left shortly after. There was a trepidation in all of his interactions thereafter which I couldn't blame him for. Surely he didn't believe my story, and he was trying to figure out what the point of it all was. As was I.

What I said to him was true, it wasn't nothing. One small piece of the puzzle is better than none. The basement was likely built with local stuff, and it was likely built long before it... became my basement. I had suspicions before, but now they were confirmed. This was the basement of a different house, somehow moved in place of mine. This left me with one ultimate burning question: Whose basement was it before?

CHAPTER IX
A Broken Record

"So whose basement was it before?" Maddy asked, after I explained what Martin found, and my hypothesis.

"My thoughts exactly." I responded.

"Well I guess that's what we have to find out. Then we can find out why, or how it's here." She said. I could tell from her voice that she was completely involved and completely invested... It almost felt too easy to get her on board like this.

"How are we supposed to do that? How can an empty basement tell us who lived there?" I posed.

"Maybe it can't... But maybe those things you've been seeing and hearing can."

I thought it just as she said it, and it all came to me in a rush.

"The names." I muttered to myself.

"The what?"

IT TAKES

"Names. I've been hearing voices and some of the voices have said names. First names, but maybe they're part of this. Can we use that somehow? Search up those names—and we know they're probably local–so those names, plus our area, and see if something comes up."

"Okay. Sure, I mean, we can try." Maddy said hesitantly.

"Yes. We can try... You do it though, you're better at that shit than me."

"Okay, what are the names?" Maddy asked, pulling out her phone.

"Jackson–no, Jacob–and Caleb."

"That's it? Those are... pretty common names, dad."

"Yeah, I know, but both together? That narrows it down."

"I feel like it probably won't..." Maddy said doubtfully as she scrolled, "I mean, I just typed it in and nothing is jumping out at me."

"Really? Shit..."

"The internet isn't a miracle worker, dad."

I thought harder about the names... I thought about the voices... I thought about the cadence of them...

"There's more..." I said.

"More?"

"It's not just the names... It's how they were said." I began to put the pieces together, "They weren't spoken TO me, none of the voices spoke to me. They were just speaking, and I was overhearing it. Echoes of conversations they've already had. That's what they feel like... And the way the names were said..."

"How were they said?"

"Jacob–it was like shock. Confusion. Fear. Like the person had been caught, or snuck up on. Caleb though... That was different. They were screaming his name. Crying. Just... wailing."

I contemplated for another moment before coming to my shaky conclusion.

"Caleb is dead. Caleb was killed. And the wailing voice, it was woman's voice. She was so... broken. I've never heard anything like it. It had to be... It had to be his mother. Which makes Caleb a child. Maybe the child I've been hearing... Maybe someone killed that child. Maybe it was in that basement."

"Dad..." Maddy interrupted, concern in her voice.

"Wait... The child... All he says is "Daddy?" Why is that all he says? And the way he says it, he's surprised. He's confused. Why would he be confused to see his dad? What is his dad doing that confuses him?"

"Dad, you're freaking me out."

"Sorry, Maddy. I'm sorry. Just... give me a second." I pleaded. My legs grew restless and I began to pace, as if that would help my brain work faster.

Whether it helped or not, the jigsaw puzzle began to form. As much as I didn't want to freak Maddy out anymore, I had to lay it out, and I had to do it now.

"I think I'm starting to get it, Mads."

"Get what?"

"Why do they only say one thing? Why do they repeat one word or phrase over and over? People always say ghosts are trapped. They're 'doomed to relive their final moments'. That's always the thing with ghosts, right? That's what ghosts are. The last vestiges of us, the last memories, played on a loop. All of these words... Maddy... They're final words. They're the last thing these people said before they died. And the last thing the child said was "Daddy?" Don't you see? People died in that basement. People were... killed... in that basement. That's what you have to look for."

Maddy looked at me, incredulous and frightened, "Okay, dad. I'll look."

"Do you believe me?" I asked.

"I... don't know what to believe. But I want to figure this out too, so I'll look into everything tonight."

"Thank you Mads."

"Yeah... Just try and take it easy, okay?"

She was right, as always. I was a mess. I was strung out. This whole thing was beginning to consume me. We didn't talk about anything else. I didn't ask her how school was. I didn't ask about her day. I didn't ask about her friends. But then again, I rarely did ask; and she never really told me anyways. There always seemed to be something else in the way.

What came first: her not telling, or me not asking?

I used to say "I love you" every day before school and before bed too, but then she got older and she stopped saying it back. That kind of direct affection started making her feel awkward, so I stopped saying it as much too. Should I have kept saying it? I didn't know...

She was okay though, I knew she was. She was so strong. She didn't even need me around. I needed her more than she needed me. That was the problem.

***

I played with Sammy for a while. I tried to delicately broach the subject of the basement, the TV, and The Sharp Man to him, but he was disinterested in talking about it. I wondered why...

As the sun began to set, I didn't feel at ease per say, but I felt a bit more at ease than I had been previously. The answers I got, or at least the ones I surmised, told me a lot. If these were just spirits caught in their final moments, then there was no malice. We weren't targeted by some kind of tangible evil; we were merely the subject of some extradimensional... anomaly.

I thought about every encounter to this point. Looking beyond the fear I felt, straight to the facts. The fact is they never did anything to harm us. Not that I could see. Maybe nothing was out to get us, and these things just wanted to talk. They wanted their stories told. They probably wanted closure.

Their voices were seared onto my brain and I felt bad for them. There was so much pain in them. I couldn't imagine what it must be like to be stuck like that. All traces of who you used to be, reduced to a few words. No love, no memory, no past, no future, just a broken record of the scariest moment of your life. Maybe if I could give them that closure... maybe that was how this ends.

IT TAKES

A plan began to formulate in my head. I wanted to communicate with them properly. I had been avoiding them all this time, when maybe all I had to do was listen.

Sammy was already out like a light. I couldn't leave him alone, which meant I had to tell Maddy. I hoisted his body up from his bed and carried him over to Maddy's door.

"I need to drop Dummy off here for a little bit, alright?"

"What are you doing?" Maddy asked.

"I'm going to try to talk to them." I responded, dropping Sammy on her bed.

Maddy's eyes widened, "What do you mean? Who?"

"The fuckin..." I answered while vaguely gesturing with my hand.

"Ghosts?"

"Or whatever they are." I added.

"Oh..." Maddy's expression dropped slightly. Her tone was slightly off in a way that I didn't know how to acknowledge.

"Yeah... I think I know how to communicate with them. If I can find out what they want, maybe I can help them."

"You want to help them?"

"Yeah, then maybe they'll leave. I don't think they mean us harm."

"Are you... sure about that?" Maddy asked, with a deep twist of unease beneath her voice. One I was unaccustomed to.

I had the chance to lie. To employ the dad bravado. I chose not to this time.

"No. I'm not sure of anything. This just feels like what I have to do."

"Okay... Well I'm coming then." Maddy asserted.

"No. Absolutely not. I need you to stay with Sam."

"I think... we should all stay together." Maddy said, almost pleading. I had to ask.

"Maddy... Is everything okay?"

"I'm fine."

I could see it behind her eyes clear as day, she was afraid. I began to suspect that it wasn't just from what I had been telling her.

"You... believed me." I began to theorize out loud, "When I started talking about voices and ghosts and shit... You played skeptical at first, but you went along with it pretty quickly."

Maddy shook her head and her hands began to fidget with the items on her desk.

"You've seen things, haven't you?" I prodded.

"No. I haven't seen anything like you have."

"Then why did you believe me?"

Maddy sighed, "I believed you when you told me about The Sharp Man."

"What? Why?"

"Because I know what that means."

Once again the hair on the back of my neck stood on end. My mind raced and I struggled to get more words out.

"W—What are you talking about?"

IT TAKES

"You weren't here, you were at work. I was watching Sammy. This was maybe two years ago... He was running around like an asshole, you know how he was."

I nodded.

"Somehow—and I don't know how—he gets a hold of a steak knife."

"What!?" I yelled.

"I know. This is why I didn't tell you. Anyways, he's running around with this knife. I try to grab it from him before he fucking dies, and he accidentally slices my hand. Nothing super deep but, it hurt... But he doesn't know what the hell anything means, he's laughing. I get the knife from him and I just point at it and yell "SHARP!" and then I point at the cut on my hand and yell "SHARP!" again and again. Trying to... I don't know... create word association. I was panicking. But ever since then, every time he sees a cut or a scar he points at it and says "sharp.""

"THAT'S why he does that?"

"Yeah. That's why. And I haven't seen any of these things like you have, not while I'm awake. But for the past five nights in a row I've had a dream about a man with cuts all over his face and a giant split down the middle of his head."

I had no idea what to say. My mental image of this man she described was instantly horrific.

Maddy continued. "So, I don't know if I can believe that these things don't mean us harm. Maybe they are just lost souls like you said, repeating their final moments. But if that's true, I don't want to know what that thing's final moments were. And I really don't want to know why he was smiling."

"Jesus, Maddy."

"I don't think you should try to talk to them, dad."

"I know, but I have to figure this out. This is all the more reason to do it. They're talking to me regardless; I just need to be able to hear them better. We're so close. If we get one or two more names, maybe we can put it all together. That's all we need."

I saw Maddy's expression of disapproval and fear, so I came up with a compromise. "Okay here's what you can do. You can stay at the top of the stairs while I go down. That way you've got one eye on the kid, and I can shout if I need anything. Alright? We won't be apart."

Maddy relented, "Okay."

IT TAKES

CHAPTER X
THEY ARE HIS

The plan was simple enough. The voices came through best on the old TV. I figured that the signal would be stronger if I put the TV in the epicentre of this whole thing.

I made my way briskly through the house. I could hear the wind begin to whistle through the walls. Through the living room window I could see the snow starting to pick up, but I didn't have time to fret about that now.

I grabbed an extension cord and plugged it in on an upstairs outlet before throwing the rest down into the abyss. Then I took a desk lamp from the living room, brought it down. I connected it and set it on the concrete floor, illuminating a small patch at the staircase's end.

Finally I hauled my big, fat CRT down the stairs. I sat it dead in the center of the big empty space, and plugged it in as well. Maddy tossed the flashlight down afterwards and I was ready to begin.

IT TAKES

I sat cross legged in front of the small, dark screen. Neither the light from the lamp, nor the small amount coming in from the upstairs door was enough to reach all the dark corners of the basement. Though I could see just well enough to notice that my breath was visible.

I switched the TV on and was faced with the familiar static and the loud, crackling hiss that accompanied it. More than loud enough to drown out the old familiar tick tock. The more my eyes adjusted to the blinding white light, the more the rest of the room cascaded into darkness. Was this a bad idea? Was I doing the right thing? I didn't know. All I knew was that I was terrified.

"Tell me who you are." I requested softly. "Tell me why you're here."

I attuned myself to the static. I gave in to its hypnotic effects, hoping that bringing the TV down here would increase the connection to whatever it was.

The first few minutes yielded nothing, but I was patient. Determined.

"Daddy?" the familiar child's voice broke through the static. My body shook to attention.

"Caleb. Is that you? Is that your name?" I called out, still attempting to speak softly.

"Daddy?" it repeated.

"What happened to you, Caleb?" I asked, allowing more urgency to enter my tone.

"Daddy?"

"Where is your daddy? What did he do?"

"Daddy?"

I sighed. He didn't seem able to say anything else. I didn't even know if he could hear me or understand me. Maybe this wasn't going to be a conversation, maybe it was just a broken record after all.

"I'm sorry." The solemn voice from before echoed through the static, and the other voices slowly came with it. Every minute or so, one would come through. I listened intently to see if there was any more clarity.

"No!" "I don't want to." "Jacob!" "Daddy?" "Caleb!" "The house." "I remember." "Why am I here?" All phrases I've heard before, but thinking of them as the final words of these poor souls stuck out of time cast a deep feeling of dread over me.

I wondered who these people were. What their lives were like. What happened to them... Which of these words belonged to The Sharp Man...

"Can't see." Wait... That was a new one.

"Even without you." A different new voice. Quieter and barely perceptible.

"Not you, the other one."

"Tell my dad."

"Help!" A blood curdling feminine scream broke through the static, sending a jolt through my body.

"Always wins."

"It wasn't supposed to be like this."

The voices began to get louder and more frequent, like they were trying to break through. Every minute became every 10 seconds, became every second. Voices looping and layering atop one another. Noise on top of noise.

IT TAKES

"Daddy?" "I don't want to." "I'm sorry." "Always wins." "Make it stop." "Tell my dad." "The other one." "Darren?" "Jacob!" "Brooke." "They are his." "Can't see." "Not you." "Even without you." "Tell my dad." "Daddy?" "Darren?" "Brooke." "Caleb!" "I'm sorry." "The other one." "Always wins." "Tell my dad." "The house." "Always wins." "The house." "Always wins."

"The house always wins."

"The house always wins."

"The house always wins."

"The house always wins."

"The house always wins."

"Dad!" Maddy's voice startled me from the top of the staircase. I wanted to turn away from the TV to respond but I had to keep listening.

"Daddy?" "Even without you." "Make it stop." "Other one." "Not you."

"They are his."

"They are his."

"They are his."

"Without you." "They are his."

"They are." "Without you."

"Dad! Get up here!" Maddy pleaded. I heard her. I heard the urgency in her voice. I wanted to move, but I was transfixed. I couldn't take my eyes away. Just a little more.

"Don't want." "To be." "Here."

"Don't" "Be" "Here"

"Daddy" "Even" "Make" "Other" "Not"

"Daddy" "Even" "Make" "Other" "Not"

A hand grabbed me violently by the arm and I jolted out of my daze. It was Maddy.

"Dad! We have to go!" She shouted. I slowly stood up, my eyes were stinging worse than ever.

"What's happening?" I asked frantically.

"It's Sammy, it's... it's..." She trailed off as she slowly looked towards the screen. Her eyes widened.

"What? Maddy, what? What happened?" I shouted, trying to get her attention back, but she just stared towards the snow.

"Oh my god... I hear them... I hear them all..." Maddy whispered. Tears began forming in her eyes.

"Maddy!"

"The house always wins..." Maddy said curiously, trying to discern the words. "I'm sorry... You are his... The other one..."

"Maddy!" I shouted again, pulling her shoulders away and turning her to face me, "What happened to Sammy!?"

After a moment, I saw her consciousness come back online and she answered with tears flowing down her cheeks, "The Sharp Man."

IT TAKES

CHAPTER XI

THE DRAGON BEHIND THE DOOR

I rushed up the stairs to the sounds of Sammy screaming in horror. I darted down the hallway towards it and when I stood in the doorway to Maddy's room, I saw him. He was laid out on the bed, screaming and convulsing.

"I don't know what happened, he was sleeping and then..." Maddy explained through tears.

"SAM!" I yelled as I made my way to the bed side. I saw that his eyes were closed. I held his body down to the bed to stop the violent thrashing. His screams pierced through me.

"SHARP!" "SHARP!" He screamed.

"It's okay! It's okay! Sammy, you're dreaming!" I shouted, but the screams continued. He wouldn't stop shaking and flailing in my arms.

"What do we do!?" Maddy yelled through the chaos.

Thinking quickly, I instructed Maddy "Get the book!"

IT TAKES

"What book?"

"The dragon one. The one he likes. The one that you always put him to sleep with."

Maddy quickly ran out of the room and returned a few seconds later holding the children's book.

"Come here. Read it to him."

Maddy knelt down beside me, opened the book to a random page and began reading softly into his ear.

"The dragon's belly gurgled. "So hungry!" He snapped. "Why must I be confined to this awful trap?" He looked for a way–any way to be freed, so he could continue his insatiable greed."

I felt Sammy's body begin to tire and his screams began to soften. It was working.

"The brave knight entered, not keen to be a meal. But to his surprise, the dragon offered a deal. "Set me free now, let me soar in the skies. In return, dear knight, I shall give you a prize." The knight knew better, he knew it was a jape. There was no way he could let the dragon escape."

His breathing began to regulate. Pretty soon he was completely calm. Maddy and I both let out a huge sigh of relief. Sammy's eyes slowly began to open.

"Thank god." Maddy said under her breath.

"Maddy!" Sam yelled, wrapping his arms around her and crying into her shoulder. I wrapped my arms around both of them.

"I don't want The Sharp Man to take me! Please don't let him take me!" Sammy cried.

"You just had a bad dream, kid. It's okay." Maddy said in her most soothing voice.

Maddy looked towards me and I saw everything she wanted to say written in her pleading expression. She wanted us to leave.

"We're gonna go to a motel for the night, okay?" I said to the both of them. Then I added directly to Maddy, "We'll figure it out from there."

She nodded. I walked into my room to begin preparing an overnight bag, but then I looked out the window. My heart began to sink.

I walked over to the living room window to get a better view of the driveway, and that confirmed it.

We were snowed in, and it was still coming down hard. It would take all night to clear the driveway, and even then, the roads likely wouldn't be plowed until much later. We were stuck.

Maddy and Sammy joined me in the living room, they both saw what I saw. Maddy's expression instantly dropped.

"Okay." I said, formulating a new plan. I turned to Sammy. "Here's what we're gonna do. We're gonna have a slumber party! Here in the living room, the three of us."

"I can stay up?" Sammy asked.

"You can stay up, you can sleep, you can do whatever you want because there's no school tomorrow! We'll bring your bed out here, and your favorite toys. Until the snow goes away, we're all gonna stay in the living room." I turned to Maddy, "Sound good?"

Maddy nodded again. Sammy cheered. It wasn't ideal, but it was something.

IT TAKES

I began getting to work setting the living room up for us, while also quickly grabbing the TV out of the basement so I could shut and barricade the door with the chair once again. Unsure of how much it would help at this point, but just one extra measure.

Sammy didn't want to go back to sleep for the first couple hours, so we played some games and put on a movie.

We had a full on Connect Four tournament that we let him win.

It was fun... It had been so long since we all had fun together like this. I couldn't figure out why I didn't make this happen more often. There was just always something else in the way.

Eventually he passed out again. Maddy and I watched over him in the dim lamp light.

"Should we take turns sleeping?" Maddy asked.

"Yeah, that's probably the move."

A few moments of silence followed between us, before a question formed in my head.

"Those dreams you had, about that... guy. What exactly happened in them? Was there anything else?"

Maddy paused before answering, "Uh, yeah. I mean they were strange. I didn't think much about them at the time." She shifted in her seat, "They start with me, walking through the house at night. Then I come to a door in the hallway. I can't tell which door, but when I open it it's just... blackness. The floor is made of fog, and it goes on forever. Then someone takes my hand. I look up and it's him. He's wearing this... elegant suit—this tuxedo. But he has cuts all over his face. Bleeding from every one, I can almost see his skull through the giant gash down the middle of his head. He's smiling at me... I'm scared but then..."

"Then what?"

"Then... Suddenly I'm in this fancy white dress. He brings me in and we start dancing. Slow dancing, in this void. I don't want to but my body moves anyway. I feel the blood from his face trickle down mine. And there's this echo... It's like people singing in an opera, but it's so far away. We dance to it, and... suddenly I'm happy. I don't know why but I am. Like everything else just falls away. Then I turn around and... well... I see mom."

"Your mom is there?"

"Yeah... She's standing there watching us dance. Then she holds her arms open and I start walking towards her... Then I wake up."

I took a minute to process, unsure of what to say, "...Wow. That's... a lot."

"Yeah, I don't know what it means. If it means anything."

I sat back and shrugged. Letting the silence fill the space. I didn't know if I should pry into her feelings about her mother.

"Do you still hate her?" Maddy asked.

I was taken aback, she never asked anything like that before.

"No. No, I've never hated her." I answered, honestly. That answer seemed to be enough for her, she decided not to follow up.

IT TAKES

It was the truth. I didn't hate her for leaving us. She tried. She did. But those last few months after Sammy was born, I knew she was gone. I knew one night I'd wake up and she wouldn't be there. I even heard her get up in the middle of the night and pack her things, and I didn't stop her. I figured it would be better to let her go than to force her to stay.

Maybe I was wrong for that. Maybe I was wrong for a lot of things.

CHAPTER XII

The Axe Man

We sat in that silence, somewhere between comfortable and uncomfortable for a few more minutes, until I figured it was time enough.

"Alright." I said, leaning over, grabbing my laptop and handing it to Maddy. "You got work to do."

Maddy pinched her eyes and sniffed, "Uh, right. Yeah, let's do it."

"I got more names."

"Good... Okay..." Maddy commented while opening and preparing the laptop. "Go."

"Darren, Brooke... yeah... Caleb, Jacob, Darren, and Brooke." I listed. "And make sure you add some keywords like 'tragedy' or 'murder' – oh and the location, because the house is probably local."

"Yeah, yeah, I got it." Maddy said, already typing.

IT TAKES

I let her have at it, as I diverted my attention between her and Sammy. He was still out. No signs of a nightmare or anything else.

I listened as the wind outside ravaged and it filled me with a dark feeling. Until now, leaving had been an option. Until now, if worse came to worse I could at least gather them up in the car and drive away some place. Until now...

I checked the clock. To my surprise, it was only a little after midnight. I had hoped it was later. The thought of 8 more hours of darkness was deeply distressing.

"Dad." Maddy called out after about 15-20 minutes of sleuthing.

"Yeah?"

"I think I got something..."

I was instantly alert, "Really?"

Maddy began to pass me the laptop, "Read this."

I sat it on my lap and my eyes adjusted to the screen. I was faced with an older looking website. It featured a sky blue background with basic black Times New Roman text that was only a little hard to read.

At the top, a banner written in early aughts-era Word Art which read "Maritime Mysteries!" Along with a few clipart images of boat helms and anchors. Below it, the title of the article which I read out loud.

"'Ashbrooke House: Nova Scotia's Murder Manor' – sounds promising." I muttered.

"Keep reading." Maddy insisted impatiently.

A.W. SCHOFIELD

It was clunky and unprofessional looking, but oddly that made me trust it. This was clearly a passion project. I began silently reading the unformatted wall of text.

"Throughout history, there have been places that seem to attract tragedy: The Cecil Hotel, Aokigahara Forest, Hawthorn Woods; but there is another location, dear readers, that not many know about and it lives... right under our noses." Good enough start. Bit cheesy. The next few paragraphs seemed like fluff so I skimmed over them and dug into the meat of the article.

"The first tragic event on record would occur shortly after the house's construction in 1956, when the first owner—a 58 year old woman named Catharine Ivy Smith– suffered a brain aneurysm in the house's basement and died. Less than two years later, 46 year old Brent O'Malley would also perish in the very same spot due to a carbon monoxide leak. Only one year after that, 27 year old Julia Fairsview would die by falling down the basement stairs. In the eyes of many, this solidified the house's reputation as "cursed." Further owners would even talk of seeing the ghosts of those departed roaming around the house."

I gave Maddy an unsure glance, and she returned it with one of absolute certainty. Her eyes simply said "Keep fucking reading." So I did.

"The tragedies did not end with accidents, however, as on September 9th, 1963 A man by the name of Bill Leterrier brutally murdered his son Caleb..." That name smacked me in the face. I was right. The child was Caleb. The child was murdered by this father.

IT TAKES

I continued, "...and wife Joanne with an axe. When officers arrived on the scene after a neighbour's 911 call, they would find Bill covered in blood with cuts all over his person, determined to have been caused by shards of a broken bathroom mirror. Whether from a struggle, or self-inflicted–nobody knows. Bill would chillingly utter the words "The house always wins" before slamming his own face into the sharp edge of his axe until dead. The bodies of Caleb and Joanne were found in the basement."

The hair on the back of my neck stood on end. This was it. Ashbrooke House was the place. Caleb was the child. Bill Leterrier was The Sharp Man. Maddy did it. We have our lead.

I could feel Maddy anxiously studying my reaction. I decided to read on.

"From that event onwards, talk of the house's curse spiked. Reports of paranormal incidents would skyrocket. Many future owners would flee the house with little explanation. Curiously, beyond the events that took place within the house, Ashbrooke was also home to multiple individuals who would go on to commit terrible crimes elsewhere. Darren Barbeau, Jacob Adams, and Fraser Caine had all stayed in Ashbrooke House at one point or another in their youth. Whether they had committed any of their crimes inside the house is unknown."

Those names each had their own hyperlinks. I could only imagine what I would learn if I clicked them, but I had no desire to go down more rabbit holes at the moment. I got the picture... Part of it anyway.

"That's it, isn't it?" Maddy asked, seeing that I had finished reading.

"That's it... Holy shit, that's it." I exclaimed, "See if you can find the address." I added, passing the laptop back.

As cathartic as it was to finally solve this crucial piece of the puzzle, it did leave me with two new burning questions, that I chose not to share.

Number one, there were only five deaths mentioned in that article, so where did the rest of the voices come from? I heard dozens.

Number two is... why? Why did Bill Leterrier kill his family? Why did multiple murderers live in that house? Why did he say "The house always wins?" Is there something else in that house, something even worse than The Sharp Man himself?

"Shit." Maddy said, taking me out of my mental wandering. She began to read aloud from the screen. "Edit: The address of Ashbrooke House has been removed at the request of the house's current owner, David Wyatt. We have agreed to respect their privacy and urge all others to do the same."

"Shit... Wait so someone lives there right now?" I pondered.

"Apparently."

"Interesting... Might have to talk to that David Wyatt then."

"I'll work on that."

"Thanks, Mads." I said, standing up from the couch. "Just going to the bathroom quick, watch the kid."

IT TAKES

I was dreading this inevitable trip. Leaving the relative safety of the open living room, going down that dark hallway, past that damn door. I resolved to be as quick as possible.

I walked briskly down the hall, into the bathroom. Feeling somewhat safe in the bright light. My mind anticipated something to happen, but I was able to finish up quickly.

I washed my hands, but... over the sound of the running water a heard the faintest little sharp clink. Instantly familiar but it took me a second to recall why.

Then, before getting the chance, a tiny sliver of mirror fell past my hands into the sink... Just as it had before.

It happened again. But what did it mean?

Puzzled, I looked up to see if this time I could determine its point of origin.

Instead I screamed.

Staring back at me from the mirror wasn't my own face. I knew exactly whose face it was. Blood pooled in his toothy smile as it cascaded down from a multitude of long, deep cuts. He had long, patchy, wispy hair that looked like he had torn most of it out. His skin pulled and twisted to the whim of the slits in his flesh creating unnatural curvatures. One of his eyelids was severed completely. The split down the middle of his face... That enormous gash from the axe he had turned on himself... it went so deep it was like a perpetually oozing cavern.

I turned to run out of the bathroom, dripping the handle tight, but the door was stuck. I pulled and I pulled, getting nowhere, until I heard a loud, shattering crash behind me.

I looked back and the mirror was shattered. Full of jagged cracks not unlike the ones on his face.

And The Sharp Man was gone. I gasped and yelled out again as I pounded and tugged on the door.

Before long I heard commotion on the other side, "Dad!" Maddy shouted.

I felt her pulling at the door from her end. I looked back once more and the shatter marks began to bleed. Agonizingly slow drips of deep, thick crimson weaving in and out of each crack on the way down.

Then the door finally gave way. I nearly crashed into Maddy.

"Fuck!" I shouted, "Jesus Fucking Christ."

"What happened!?"

I ignored her question and grabbed her arm to run her back to the living room.

"Wait!" she exclaimed. "Where's Sammy?"

My heart skipped a beat. "What do you mean, where's Sammy?"

"I didn't want to leave him alone in the living room, so I woke him up and brought him with me! He was right beside me! I was holding on to him!"

"No. No no no no no. Shit." I uttered, now panicking even more. I instantly walked to the basement. The chair was still propped up in front of it, but that didn't deter me from thinking he somehow got down there. That was still the most likely option. How could he get down there so

IT TAKES

fast and put the chair back? I didn't care anymore. Nothing was off the table.

"Check the living room, check the bedrooms. I'm going down." I instructed. "Yell everywhere you go. Yell so I can hear."

"Okay, dad. Be careful." She pleaded.

I moved the chair and opened the door. I was smart enough to keep the flashlight on me this time.

I briskly walked down the narrow basement steps. The cold wasted no time taking its hold of me.

"SAM!" I screamed, pointing the flashlight in all directions. The damn ticking sound made its presence heard.

"He's not in the living room!" Maddy yelled, just loud enough for me to hear.

I moved the flashlight around every inch, but I saw nothing. He had to be here, I thought. This was always the place. Where else would he be?

"He's not in my room!" Maddy yelled down once again.

"SAM!" I repeated to no avail.

"DAD!" Maddy screamed. Her voice was full of horror. My heart leapt into my throat and I ran back up the stairs. I looked to my right and saw Maddy standing outside the door to Sammy's room.

"What is it!?"

Tears were streaming down Maddy's face as she merely pointed into the room. I ran over and looked inside. The window was wide open.

A.W. SCHOFIELD

IT TAKES

CHAPTER XIII
THE COLD ALONE

The next 5 minutes were a whirlwind. Sammy was nowhere to be found, his bedroom window which had been locked, was now wide open and blowing snow inside.

Maddy was crying, but we weren't without hope. All of that snow had in this moment been a godsend. I could see his tracks through the window go into the woods behind our house.

But I didn't have much time. He couldn't survive out there for long.

"Call the police, and wait here." I instructed Maddy while I quickly flung my winter coat on. Without hesitation I saw her wipe her tears away and get her phone out. I slid on my winter boots, grabbed the flashlight and ran out the front door before I could hear her make the call.

IT TAKES

I made my way around the side of the house to Sammy's window and began to follow the child size boot prints.

I sprinted after them, shouting Sammy's name over and over again. The snow was beginning to come down even harder and the wind was blowing fast. The tracks still looked fresh, but it wouldn't be long before they were covered.

The tracks didn't seem to end. He must have been running too. Running from what? I looked back, and I couldn't see the light of my house anymore. Nor the light of anything, except my flashlight against the blanket of white. The jacket and boots didn't offer as much protection from the elements as I had hoped. Nights like this required so much more. The cold was biting me hard.

I must have been running for 20 minutes, only ever briefly stopping for a breath, desperate to catch up to the poor boy who must have been freezing.

I couldn't bear the thought. Maddy said he was right beside her, so he couldn't have gotten his coat before he climbed out of that window. He snuck out into the snow in his damn pajamas. Didn't even have his...

Boots.

I stopped, looking at the tracks before me. Small boots... Definitely boots. I saw Sammy's boots by the door. Another thing I saw without seeing. But they were definitely there.

This wasn't Sammy. So whose tracks were these? The child, Caleb? But why?

Why? I pondered, the word spinning in my head like a washing machine... But then it hit...

To get me away from the house.

It was a trick.

Fuck, I had left Maddy alone in that goddamn house.

I turned back around and ran once again, hoping that the tracks would remain long enough to find my way home. I wanted to run faster but I could only trudge.

The snow got heavier and heavier. The wind nearly knocked me on my ass. This wasn't just heavy snow anymore, this was a blizzard. A bad one.

My face began to sting and my extremities started going numb. My chest pounded. The relentless wind fought me every step. The snow felt like needles against my skin. I was wholly unprepared.

I began doing the math. I ran nonstop for about 20 minutes. At the rate I was moving now, it was gonna take at least twice as long to get back. That is, if it didn't get worse—and if I didn't get lost.

Unfortunately, both of those things happened.

The snow reached my knees, and it showed no signs of slowing. The tracks were gone. I was running out of time.

It wasn't long before I felt like I was going to die, and it was becoming a scarily real possibility. Is this what they wanted? Had they all been plotting this? Even the child?

All of their jumbled-up words and phrases replayed in my mind. I hadn't had a chance to try and make sense of them. They wanted so desperately to communicate with me. They were trying to warn me. Why would they warn me if they wanted to kill me? That didn't add up. It must have been something else.

I trudged further and further. I couldn't feel my face anymore, and my legs desperately wanted to give out, but I couldn't allow them to.

What were they warning me of? What were they trying to tell me? I was missing something. Something itching at the back of my mind. What was it? What did I miss?

"The house always wins." Were they all part of 'the house'? Did it have some power over them? Were they not in control?

My body was shutting down. My hand couldn't grasp the flashlight anymore, it just slipped from my fingers and buried into the snow. I stuffed my numb hand into my jacket pocket, hoping to give it some chance at regaining feeling, but the damage was done. My toes were gone too. The snow no longer melted when it hit my face. It just stuck there. Piling on. Forming a crust.

Everything was slowing down to a crawl. It took a monumental effort to even remain upright. It took almost the same amount of effort to keep my eyes open in the constant barrage of snow hitting me like a shotgun.

"Just don't stop moving." I thought to myself, "If you stop, you die." But it was so hard now. Was I even close to being home? Once I got home, what could I do in this state? What could I possibly do if Maddy was in danger?

Maddy... I failed her. Not just today but so many times. I put Sammy first... I put him first because he needed me more. But they both needed me. They both needed more than me.

Somewhere in the second hour, I collapsed. My feet gave way and I dropped to my knees. My numb hands plunged into the snow. I couldn't get up. I physically couldn't. But I couldn't stop either. I had to keep moving. So I crawled...

I finally closed my eyes. I didn't suppose it mattered much to be able to see anymore.

When they shut, I saw Maddy. She was 12 years old, peering at me from the bathroom door. I knew exactly what memory this was. I hated this memory.

Maddy was always a bit of a handful as a kid. The preteen years were particularly ugly. Especially after her mom left... How do you explain that? How could I possibly fill that void?

She blamed me for Steph leaving. She told me constantly that she was going to go live with her. That one day mom was gonna come pick her up.

Every day that didn't happen, she resented me even more. I couldn't fix it. I couldn't be her mother. I couldn't be what she needed me to be, especially since I had a screaming 9-month-old baby that I had to make not die on top of all that.

IT TAKES

But I'm a parent. So that's what you do. You push it down, and you do the impossible. But above all, you never let them see the damage.

But I wasn't good enough. I wasn't strong enough. There was this one day. This one damn day I just ran out of steam. I sat on the floor of the bathroom, with this screaming infant in my arms... I can't even remember what it was that set me over the edge but it all came to the surface and I broke down. I cried, and I sobbed, and I wailed. It was too much. It was too hard. I couldn't do it.

Then I saw her face, peeking in the bathroom door. Staring at me. I'll never forget the look on her face. The look in her eyes. She was never supposed to see me like that.

From that moment on, she never complained again. She never acted out. She never yelled. She started helping out around the house. She started helping take care of Sammy and... it was great. I was so proud of her. All it cost was her childhood...

I failed her that day. I let her see the damage. And then I failed her every single day since by accepting all of her help.

It was selfish. If I was a better dad, she wouldn't have to sacrifice so much... she could still be a kid. But I took that from her, I forced her to grow up, because I wasn't good enough. Because I couldn't hack it.

Every day I wished she would just ask me for something. One thing. One favor. Ask me for help. I wish she would be difficult or be angry. Nag me for things like she used to. Disobey, get into mischief. That's what kids are supposed to do. But that part of her died, because of me.

Now I've exposed her to this too. I brought her in and made her a part of this... because I still couldn't hack it.

I was dying. I knew it. I failed again. I failed the only people I have. The only people I care about in this world.

But suddenly I felt something under my arm. An edge. Leading to something hard, but smoother than the ground. It creaked as I put weight on it. I managed to force my eyes open to make sure I wasn't mistaken.

The steps, leading up to the porch. I made it. I actually made it. It took every bit of energy I had left to hoist myself up the stairs. Even more to reach the doorknob and somehow open it without use of my fingers, but I managed.

The door swung open with my limp body against it and I collapsed into the safety of my home. From the floor I kicked the door closed behind me and then I laid, waiting for the warmth to reach me, if it ever would.

IT TAKES

CHAPTER XIV

CRICKETS

It took forever for me to even begin feeling again. In the meantime, I mustered up the lung power to shout.

"Maddy!"

No answer... No cops either. What happened? Did she not call? Could they just not reach us in this weather?

"MADDY!"

Still nothing... What have I done?

"MADDY!? SAMMY!? WHERE ARE YOU!?" I shouted, my voice cracking and stumbling with every word.

The house was quiet. The only sound was the whistling of the gale force outside and the creaks of the structure struggling to withstand it.

I crawled through the living room, down the long hallway, and into the bathroom. I crawled through the broken glass of the mirror and climbed into the tub, letting the showerhead rain warm water upon me.

The warmth gradually enveloped me and pierced through the numbness. My fingers and toes began to move again. I was elated that they weren't gone for good, but that didn't stop the tears from flowing.

Just like that night all those years ago, I broke. How could I not? Both of their faces tormented my thoughts. They trusted me, and I let them both down.

I gave myself until my muscles came back online to indulge in my breakdown. Then I had to stuff it all back deep inside, and fix it.

The strength in my legs took longer to come back, but eventually I could stand unaided.

I exited the bathroom in my dripping wet clothes and immediately headed for the basement. I didn't know what my plan was, but down there was my only bet.

I flung the door open, which took more effort than I was expecting. I was still far too weak.

The abyss stared up at me. Pitch black. My flashlight was buried. I had no way of seeing, but I went down anyway.

Step after step, my senses heightened. I didn't know what I hoped to find.

I tripped on the last step. Too weak to recover or brace myself, I fell directly on my face against the cold concrete. A dull pain shot through me.

"Fuck." I exclaimed out loud. I miscounted the steps.

...Or, maybe I didn't. Something didn't feel right.

I slowly got up to my feet, feeling my muscles throb and pop. I lurched forward, only to trip once again. This time only down to a knee.

Some object was in my way. It crinkled and I heard the jingling of zippers, I assumed some kind of suitcase or overnight bag.

I moved my hands around the space cautiously and connected with more random objects. Plastic, fabric, cardboard. Things strewn about seemingly haphazardly in all directions.

"No." I thought, "It can't be."

I shuffled back towards the steps and felt along the wall for the light switch. The light switch that hadn't worked ever since the basement changed.

I found the switch and flicked it on, and my suspicions were proven correct.

The light came on. The basement... was ours. All of our stuff was back. All of our clutter. Everything was back in its rightful place once again. The steps had the correct number.

I listened closely. I heard the hum of the boiler. I didn't hear the ticking anymore.

Even that feeling, that deep foreboding, that inexplicable dread, was gone... It took with it, my hope.

What could I do now? What happened? Where were they?

I ran back up the stairs, my body in agony as I pushed it beyond its limits in a desperate stupor. I paced around the entire house. Looking for something, anything. I screamed. Over and over.

IT TAKES

"WHERE ARE THEY?"
"WHAT HAVE YOU DONE TO THEM?"
"WHAT DO YOU WANT?"
"TALK TO ME!"
"TELL ME WHAT YOU WANT!"
"GIVE THEM BACK TO ME!"
"GIVE THEM BACK!"

I shouted again and again into the air. I picked up the landline and shouted into it, praying that the voices would call out to me again, but I was only met with a dial tone. I threw the phone to the floor and then collapsed in a heap. My head throbbed. I felt swelling begin.

Out the window I could see that the snow had begun to ease, but it would still be a while before driving would be possible. Even if I knew where they were, I couldn't get there.

The thought of being stuck in this house while my kids were all alone with whatever it was made me want to scream. The utter silence felt like a sadistic taunt. A constant reminder of my failure. My powerlessness.

I wanted to just curl up and die. I wanted this all to be over somehow. I couldn't deal with this. All the thoughts of what could be happening to my children... I couldn't bear it. But one little voice remained. The same little voice that told me "Just don't stop moving." And it was saying the exact same thing now. That little voice saved me, and now I needed it to save them.

Keep moving. Don't stop. If you stop, they die.

A.W. SCHOFIELD

It doesn't matter if it's impossible. That's what you do when you're a parent. You hurt, you cry, you reach your limit, you go insane, and then you do it.

IT TAKES

CHAPTER XV
THE HOUSE

I didn't have a logical reason for why I knew my children would be at that house. But none of this had been logical from the start. The room went back to where it came from, and it took them with it. That was my conclusion.

I opened my laptop and saw the unfinished search Maddy had begun on David Wyatt–the current owner of Ashbrooke House. I had to find him. There was no way he could live in that house and not know something.

"David Wyatt, I need to talk to you about Ashbrooke House. It's urgent. Please respond." I typed, then copied and pasted into the messages of every profile with that name on every social network I knew of. Then I got out the phonebook and began making calls.

It only took about an hour for me to get a favorable response. Facebook did have its uses after all.

IT TAKES

"I have nothing to say about Ashbrooke House, please respect my privacy." The message read.

I typed back with haste, "It's an emergency. My kids are in danger. Please call me so I can explain." Then I left my cellphone number. About a minute later I received a call.

"Who are you? What happened? Is my full name still on that goddamn kid's website?" A stern, gravelly voice asked through the receiver.

I wasn't sure how to start. I wanted to explain everything from the beginning but I didn't want to waste time or lose his attention. How could I explain this when I didn't even know what was happening?

"My name is Adam, and I think my kids might be... in your basement." I cringed. That sounded so odd to say.

"What?" The voice replied, clearly dumbfounded.

I sighed, "Look... I know you know something's wrong with your house. You wouldn't have picked up the phone if you didn't. I don't know how to say this except that your house has been tormenting my family. My kids are gone. I think it took them. I need your address. I need your help."

"No..." He exclaimed, his tone weary and tinged with unease, "God damn it... Why were your kids trespassing on my property? How did they get in?"

"They weren't. We've never been near your house, any of us. One day our basement... changed. It wasn't our basement anymore. I have reason to believe it was yours. I don't know how. I don't know why. But one day, I opened the door to a room that wasn't mine, and something else came with it—it took them, and now it's gone. I need to find them."

The other end went silent for a moment, but I couldn't spare that moment so I continued. "I'm completely snowed in so it might take an hour or two for me to get there. Can you at least look for them? Can we get the cops involved?"

"I've never stepped foot in that house, Adam." David explained.

I fidgeted, "What?"

"I bought that house to let it rot. I've never been inside. I will never go inside, or allow anyone else to go inside."

His words chilled me to the core but I had to remain stoic, "Okay. So you know how dangerous it is. My kids are in there. Let me call the police."

"No police." He insisted.

"Why not?"

"They will have to break the locks to get inside. The locks mustn't be broken."

"What does that matter? I'll pay for your locks." I knew I was beginning to sound desperate but I didn't care. It was a desperate situation.

"The locks mustn't be broken!" He reasserted.

I didn't understand what he meant or why that was so important, but I believed the intent behind his words, and I knew he would not budge. "Then I'll go. You tell me how to get inside without breaking the locks."

"Adam, I strongly advise you to stay away from it. It's not what you think it is."

IT TAKES

"I don't care... I don't have a choice. You have to see that."

"Those articles you probably read online, they didn't tell you everything. If you go in there—"

"Do you have kids, David?" I cut him off.

"...I do."

"Then you know I have to get in that house. I'm not gonna stop. I can find your address some other way—there will be other records; and if you don't tell me how to get inside, I WILL break your locks. I have to get them back."

Another minute of silence on the other end, this time I let the silence sit.

"I've messaged you the address. Do what you think you have to do."

I silently clenched my fists, celebrating this one small victory, "Thank you, David."

The other end only sighed, "I really thought it was over. I thought I had starved it." David muttered in a more melancholic voice. I didn't really expect him to divulge more.

"What is it that's inside Ashbrooke? What else do you know?" I prodded. I needed to know everything I could.

"The articles talk about the deaths that occur in the house. The murders, the accidents. They don't tell you about what happened outside the house."

I heard another deep and conflicted sigh from the other end, and a throat clearing, "Adam, my daughter lived in Ashbrooke. My Hailey. About a week into her staying there she tells me she thinks it's haunted. Now, she didn't take it seriously and neither did I, it's just kiddie shit, right?

Well, two more weeks go by and she leaves the house. She shows up at my door crying. Sobbing. Now I still didn't really believe her stories, but I knew she wouldn't lie. She wasn't like that. I let her stay with me 'til we figured it out."

He paused and I heard shuffling on his end. He seemed to be trying to make himself more comfortable to tell this story.

"She never went back to that house again... She was adamant. Both feet planted, never again. I said 'okay, sweetie.' We both thought that was the end of it... but it wasn't. She... changed. I saw it every day she stayed with me. She was never the same... My Hailey was an incredibly gifted girl. Such a strong head on her shoulders—and smart. So much smarter than me. She was a nurse for god's sake. I was always so damn proud. But the girl that came back from that house... something was missing, and it only got worse. I never was much about shrinks and the like, but I sure as shit didn't know what else to do. So we had her see psychiatrists, psychologists, whatever the hell, all kinds of doctors. She got pills, 'Sertra'-this and that, nothing helped. Every day she was... less."

"I'm so sorry..." I interjected solemnly.

David ignored my comment and continued, determined to make his point, "I wake up one night and go check on her and she was gone... Dead. Slumped over her desk... She left a note next to her and I couldn't even read her handwriting—my own daughter's handwriting. Now I know folks struggle, and sometimes people put on a happy face but... Hailey wouldn't do that. If you knew

IT TAKES

her you would know, she would never. And it all started with that house.

"So I get to digging. I don't know jack about shit but I learn. It took a long time. Shit, I don't even know how many years its been now. And I'll tell you, I learned a lot, but I did not learn everything.

"I looked at the house's history, but unlike everybody else, I also looked at the history of those who left—who ran away like Hailey did.

"Sure enough, the same patterns keep coming up. Mental psychosis, sudden depression, sudden illness, physical AND psychological deterioration... Six of them ended up taking their own lives. Six. Four others were taken in other ways."

A pit formed in my stomach. I couldn't believe what I was hearing. This was so much worse than I had imagined.

"That's what it does. That's what it did to all of them. It tricks you, it torments you, it imprints itself upon you, it breaks your walls down, and then it takes. It takes your health, it takes your sanity, it takes your joy—it takes whatever it wants, whatever you value, until you are sucked dry. Withered. Unrecognizable to the people you love and the people who love you. Then you belong to it. Then it can use what remains of you to torment the next person."

"What is 'it'? A demon?" I asked.

"That's the go to I suppose. That's what I figured for a while. Now? I don't think it works like that. You wanna label it, you want to put it in a box, you want to learn its rules, but you can't. No one can. There are none. If there were rules, we wouldn't be able to understand them anyway. Certainly not me. But if you wanna know what I THINK, I'll tell you."

"Please."

"Adam, I think it is evil. I think it feeds on the misery and pain of others. I think it's a parasite. It dripped into our world the moment that first lady died in the basement. It grew like a mould in that very spot with every subsequent tragedy, until it was strong enough to inflict tragedy, to infect tragedy, and feed on it. Once it got Leterrier to kill for it, it fully crossed the threshold. Leterrier is the form it likes to use the most. The one it's most proud of."

The concept of this unknowable thing having a sense of pride in its work made me shudder. I didn't want to believe this explanation, but what alternative did I have?

David concluded his story, "I bought the house and kept it abandoned to starve it, but apparently it found a way. Because like I said, it doesn't play by our rules... It can't be understood. The only thing I know for sure is that it takes. Sometimes it takes for weeks, sometimes it takes for decades, sometimes it has a different plan for you entirely, but it will take."

It will take... Those words rang through my mind again and again, long after our conversation ended. They stuck in my head while I vigorously shoveled a path down the driveway. They stuck in my head while I tried desperately to get my car in driveable condition. They stuck in my head as I drove down the long, dark country road, headed for the address David gave me.

Trying to understand how the basement switched never failed to give me a headache, but I couldn't help thinking about it all. I had wished there was a logical explanation, but David was right. It doesn't play by our rules. It is beyond understanding. People stopped coming to it, so it had to come to them. So it just... did. Why move the whole room? Maybe it WAS the room. We knew nothing of its form. Maybe every time I walked into that basement, I was walking into its mouth.

Why us? Does it matter? Was it random? There had to be a reason the rooms looked so similar... Maybe that was the key. Maybe it could only move to a room that was similar enough... But there I was trying to put rules on it again...

No, I think it chose our basement because it knew it would drive me crazy. A completely different room? That's easy. Leave, call scientists, become famous for having the house that broke the laws of space and time.

But a room that's just a little bit different? A little bit off, in ways only I would notice? How could I not obsess? This thing—demon, parasite, whatever it may be... it was smart. It had been playing me from the beginning. It probably still was.

David agreed to meet me at the house, to give me whatever it was I needed to get inside. I was glad to have him on my side, even if I forced his hand with my threats.

I made it past the long stretch of emptiness and my car struggled not to get stuck in the snow or swerve off the road. I found my way into the small town of Coldwell. I took a left, then a right, and then I found myself on a long street, far away from the shops.

Long driveways with mailboxes were spread out generously along the street. The numbers on those mailboxes ticked down as I passed them. 412, 410, 408... I was almost there.

My steely determination began to break. My anxiety was rising. I saw the house slowly come into view, with a large dark green Jeep parked a ways out in front. David stuck to his word, though I could tell he was keeping his distance, even now.

I parked alongside him and got out, making sure to grab my spare flashlight. I saw a man step out of the Jeep at the same time. His voice fit him well. The impression I had of him in my head was almost completely correct. Salt and pepper hair fighting back baldness, a square jaw, a beer belly, some thick flannel, and a scowl that looked like his default mode.

Then I finally got a look at the house. I don't know what I expected. Of course it wasn't going to look like a haunted house, but still it was smaller than I thought it would be. It didn't tower over me, it didn't have some grand, foreboding presence... it was just a house. Quaint, two stories, still bigger than mine but... absolutely nothing special.

The only significant things about it were the barbed wire fence and the numerous signs warning against trespassers. No doubt David's doing.

"Adam." David greeted, coldly.

"David." I responded in kind.

"I don't suppose I can talk you out of this." David assumed, correctly.

IT TAKES

"No."

"Even after everything I told you."

"What would you do, man? If you had a chance to get Hailey out of there." It felt dirty invoking his deceased daughter, but I knew he had to understand.

David paused for a moment, then shook his head and reached into his jacket pocket.

He held up three keys and pointed to one of them, "Gate." Then he pointed to the second, "Front door." Finally to the third, "Basement."

I took them from him, puzzled at the simplicity of it. "That's it? So I can't break the locks but I can unlock the locks, that's not a problem?"

"It's not about the lock. It's about the belief in what a lock is." David responded, pointing to his temple.

I wanted to hurry up and get inside, but I couldn't let that statement hang.

"What the hell does that mean?"

"This thing, it's not... real. You know? A hunk of metal doesn't matter to it. The 'physical' doesn't matter. I told you it takes from us our joy and our love; these aren't *real* things. These are... concepts, feelings, abstracts, symbols, ideas. That's what this thing moves in. So I use locks, for the same reason I keep a grandfather clock in the hallway. The locks contain it to the house. The clock contains it to time."

That was a lot to absorb, even after all this. So far beyond me. Hearing this kind of existential, metaphysical language coming from such a simple, grounded looking man felt so wrong. This poor man had clearly been in the weeds for a long time. How many things had he tried and failed? How many years had it been?

"Well the lock didn't seem to work since it invaded my house." I countered.

"But it did work. It's bound to the basement, it never moved, don't you see? It was never really in your house. It just sent you a window, and you were the ones who stepped through it. Every time you stepped foot in that basement, you were here."

"What makes you so sure?"

David chuckled with legitimate amusement and threw up his hands, "Nothing. Shit, I haven't been sure of a single thing since what happened to Hailey. Look at me, I'm no scientist. I don't know anything. I've just been dealing with this shit for too damn long. I only know what I choose to believe, and its gotten me this far, for whatever it's worth."

David let out one more sigh and the smile drained from his face. "Good luck, Adam. I hope you find some peace. Make sure you lock those doors as soon as you enter and as soon as you exit. Do not leave them unlocked for longer than a minute, and do not break the locks."

He offered me a handshake and I accepted it. The look in his eyes was one of resignation. I could see that he thought he was sending me to my death. Maybe he was right.

I walked up the long dirt path to the rusty, battered chain link gate and inserted the first key into the padlock. The rickety gate gave way, and I quickly shut it behind me—being sure to lock it back up quick.

IT TAKES

Making my way up the cracked stone path onto the porch, staring down the unassuming front door, my legs threatened to give out on me. Yet the sight was so plain. Just an ordinary, wooden, white door. But it was the door to hell. The point of no return. "Abandon all hope ye who enter here."

I took a deep breath and plunged key #2 into the lock, turning it until I heard a click. It was time. Time to do what you have to do. Time to be a dad.

CHAPTER XVI
ALWAYS WINS

The inside of the house was as immediately unassuming as the outside. Aged, but not decayed. Dusty, but not filthy. It looked like any old house from the 90s. It was just cold, and empty. It lacked the personality of a house that was lived in. It was devoid of quirks, devoid of colour, devoid of life.

I tried for a light switch but got no luck. Makes sense that David didn't care to pay the electric bill, but now I had to navigate this place in the dark. Only minimal blue light shone in through the windows, but not enough to illuminate the dark corners. I immediately readied my flashlight.

I immediately noticed that I could still see my breath. No heat either. As I stepped further inside, I noticed one more thing.

Tick. Tock.

IT TAKES

I turned a corner towards the noise and I saw it sitting at the end of a hallway. The impossible grandfather clock. The noise I'd been hearing this whole time.

Did it really have such a purpose as David claimed? I suppose time can get away from you when you're not keeping track of it. But when you're forced to hear every tick, you have to exist in those moments. The rhythm like a rail to keep you grounded and moving in the right direction...

Maybe I was losing my mind.

The house didn't help. The quiet was deafening, making the clock and my thoughts only seem louder. I thought I liked quiet, but I didn't like this quiet. It was unnatural. It was purposeful.

Every dark corner made me anxious. Sure, that was unavoidable given everything I've experienced and learned but this felt different.

This wasn't anxiety about what COULD be in those shadows, this was anxiety about what I KNEW was in those shadows.

I couldn't see them, even when I shined my flashlight into the corners I saw nothing, but I knew they were there. The husks. Those poor souls who were hollowed out by this thing, then marionetted around to do its bidding. I felt their eyes on me. By extension, I felt its eyes on me. Whatever it was.

The first door I tried led to a bathroom. The mirror was shattered and stained in blood, just like mine. Can't have been the original mirror—the one that carved up

Leterrier's face all those years ago. Did it do this to scare me? Did it already know I was coming?

A sloshing noise caught my ear. I instinctively turned my flashlight towards it. It nearly flew from my hands.

The light shone through the thin shower curtain, illuminating a silhouette behind it. Sitting in the bathtub.

I froze. This felt so much different from what I had seen before. Gone was the abstract, gone was the disembodied whisper, gone was the distant haze and the non-corporeal phantasmagoria. I could feel this. I could smell it. I could damn near taste it.

Whatever was in there had weight. It occupied space. The air moved around it. Tangible. Tactile.

A ghost? A puppet? A husk? Maybe. But it was here. And it was so very real. As real as I was.

I saw the shadow of an arm raise into view and reach for the edge of the curtain to peel it back.

I still couldn't move.

As it began to pull, I could see the deep red hue of the liquid in the tub. Finally I collected myself, stuttering back out of the room and shutting the door firmly. It took everything in me not to scream.

I couldn't hold the flashlight steady, as much as I tried. My body begged to run. The hair on the back of my neck stood firm, pulling away from my skin like the strings on a marionette.

Must keep going. Can't stop.

The next door I tried led to an empty bedroom. At least it looked empty when it was this dark. I didn't want

IT TAKES

to shine my flashlight inside. There was no point. Don't be stupid. I just needed to find the basement.

I tried to close the door, but it refused. It resisted. I pulled hard, but it was as if there was someone on the other side pulling just as hard.

As I stared into the dark room, a figure began to make itself visible. First the vague fuzzy shape of a head cut out from the blackness, then the shoulders, then the rest.

It towered over me by a solid foot and a half.

It was moving, agonizingly slow, from the back of the room towards me. Not walking, just moving. The first thing I saw in any kind of detail was a long white gown. Then the pale, grey skin. Then the long black hair. I looked down and saw that her feet weren't touching the ground.

I was petrified, again. My heart pounded out of my chest. I felt it again. I felt her breathing the same air as me.

"Tell my dad..." Its soft feminine voice echoed. I remember that voice.

"Tell my dad..." It repeated.

"I—I—" I stammered.

"Tell my dad..." "I'm sorry..."

My lip quivered. It couldn't be... It couldn't be her, could it?... What did he say her name was?

"Hailey?" I whispered.

I got no answer. No acknowledgement. No break. She continued moving towards me, the exact same as she had been.

The door still wouldn't close. I just let go and ran. Tears fell from my eyes. From around the corner I heard the door creak and close on its own.

I took a second to regroup and let my heart rate come back down. I wiped my eyes and tried my damndest to shake the heartbreak I felt.

I realized I was being stupid. I didn't need to try doors to find the right one. I knew exactly what the door I was looking for looked like. It was mine, after all.

One hallway I hadn't checked, but I heard the pitter patter of small footsteps in the other direction. I wanted to find the door but... it could be Sammy. I had to follow them.

"Sammy?" I whispered as I reached the source of the footsteps. Then I heard the pitter patter behind me.

"Sam?" I whispered again. "Is that you, Sam?"

I knew in my gut it probably wasn't. It was probably the child. The husk of Caleb Leterrier, being pulled around on its strings by this thing, trying to fool me. But I still had to know for sure.

More footsteps led me into the kitchen, but I saw no one. I was clearly being toyed with. It was puppeting me even without the strings.

I was ready to go back to the doors, but then another pitter patter startled me. It startled me, because it was above me. Not muffled enough to be on the second floor.

No, it was on the ceiling. Right above my head.

I couldn't look. I really didn't want to see it. But I felt it looming over me. The way I felt the others. Just as real. Just as here. I took a few steps back and I heard the ceiling shuffle above me. Every step I took, I heard it crawl to match my position.

IT TAKES

"Daddy?" The thing above me called out. My entire body tensed. I couldn't look. It wanted me to look. It was daring me.

"Daddy?" It repeated, sounding somehow more hollow.

Suddenly I felt a heavy drip on my face. Landing on my forehead and cascading down. I couldn't help it. It was instinct. I looked.

The child was sprawled out above. Its body facing down to stare at me, but its limbs twisted backwards to cling to the ceiling like an insect.

Its face... It didn't have a face. Just a mangled, bloody, gaping chasm. The work of his father. The work of The Sharp Man.

I didn't have time to scream before it lunged down from the ceiling and crashed on top of me. I dropped to the ground, feeling its 40 or so pound frame land on my head. It didn't feel human, it felt like something that once was or wanted to be.

For a moment I was staring directly into the chasm of its face and it went deeper than I knew possible. Like it held a whole secret world inside. And maybe that was the truest mouth of hell. I closed my eyes as it clawed at me.

And then it was gone. The weight lifted, I opened my eyes. Nothing. Just another sick game. I laid there with the last of my sanity just about gone for good. Or maybe it was already gone. I slowly made my way back to my feet, and all I could do was get back to it. I still had a job to do.

Only a few more scans of the doors and I finally found the door to the basement. It was the only one that was locked, that should've been a dead giveaway.

I carefully produced the final key. There was probably no use in being quiet, I knew that it knew I was here, but I was quiet anyway. Maybe just as some base survival instinct.

I slid the key carefully into the lock. I began to turn it, but then I felt a strange and deeply unwelcome sensation.

Something else was here. Occupying the space. I could feel it, but it was different. Thicker, closer.

Then the breath on the back of my neck.

My body went stiff and all the hair on my body stood on end. A shape began to form in my peripheral vision.

A face, creeping slowly from behind me to the left side of me. Inches from my face. If I turned my eyes to the left I would look right into it. I didn't want to.

It stood there, breathing. I could hear it. I could feel the warmth on my ear. I wanted to recoil at the discomfort, but I remained stiff as a board. My hand still clasped around the key in the lock.

I didn't know why I thought it would help to stay still. I didn't know why I thought it would help not to look. But I did. It was all I could do.

"The house always wins." It spoke into my ear.

I couldn't help but recoil. Shivers involuntarily shot through me. It was too close. I turned my head and there he was, right in front of me.

IT TAKES

The man I now knew as Bill Leterrier. The Sharp Man, with his sadistic grin and gaping, bleeding gash in his head. His breath smelled like dead water.

Seeing his face in a mirror was one thing, seeing it now inches from me was a million times worse. My heart jumped into my throat. I never wanted to see that face again. Never. Especially never this close. He felt so much more real now. I screamed and fell back to the floor violently, but as soon as I did, he disappeared like his son before him.

Why did he disappear? Did this thing just want to scare me again?

Unfortunately, I got my answer as soon as my mind asked it.

I didn't let go of the key as I fell. In fact I was gripping it extremely tight. I felt the pain in my fingers and then I looked down. I now only held the head of the key. The rest of it remained lodged in the lock.

Realizing the situation, I jumped back to my feet and tried to pry the teeth of the key out of the lock with my fingers, I tried to turn it, but it was no use. It was jammed. The door would not be opened.

Not ten seconds later I heard their voices coming from the other side of the door.

"Dad?" Shouted Sammy.

"Dad!" Shouted Maddy.

"Help! Dad! Please help us!" They called out to me over and over, desperately.

"Sammy! Maddy! I've got you!" I yelled back, before reassessing the situation.

I had to get to them. I had to. And I knew in that very moment that I was playing right into its hands. I knew what I was about to do was EXACTLY what it wanted me to do. EXACTLY what I was told over and over again not to do. But I had no choice.

It won.

I stepped back and booted the door near the handle. It didn't budge much. I kicked it again, not much better. On the third kick I heard wood begin to snap and I saw an indentation. Two more kicks and the frame began to bust. Then I took another step back and ran at the door with my shoulder. It gave way. I did it. I broke one of the locks.

I ran; past the pieces of door, down the steps and into that old familiar basement. Into that pitch black darkness, the only light being the dull beam of my flashlight.

It was different down here. It wasn't as quiet, or as dead as it was before.

The air felt different. Heavier. More humid. There was a persistent droning noise. Some kind of hollow hum that reverberated through the walls and the floor.

Everything I shined my flashlight on glistened just a little bit more than it should, but it wasn't wet. It wasn't quite damp either. Everything was just... clammy. I knew I had to get out of here as quickly as possible.

"Sam? Madison?" I called out again. I shone my flashlight around the room. It looked empty, until I looked in the dark corners.

Sammy. He was standing in the back left corner, facing the walls. I almost didn't see him. I turned to the right and Maddy was standing similarly in the opposite corner. Both unmoving.

"Guys. It's me. It's dad. Come on now, we have to go." I reached out to them, but I had a feeling they couldn't hear me.

The low hum I was hearing began to change. Through the droning I heard the voices again. All of them, saying their final words. But it wasn't chaotic like before. It was organized. It was almost rhythmic. Their words formed some kind of chant. Melding and molding the phrases into some other kind of language.

"Sammy, come on!" I walked towards my son and placed a hand on his shoulder. He still didn't move. He was cold. I turned him to face me and his eyes were closed. His body was limp, his head swiveled as I tried to shake him awake. It felt like he wasn't even standing under his own power.

"SAM!" I shouted, trying to break through whatever was happening to him.

"You chose him." Maddy's voice let out in a whisper from across the room. The chanting quieted as she spoke.

"What?" I asked.

"But you always do, don't you."

"What are you talking about?" I asked shakily. I pointed the flashlight towards her, and she remained in the corner. Never moving an inch. I couldn't even tell if her mouth moved when she talked.

"You're a failure. You were always a failure, as a husband and as a father." She muttered.

"Maddy, we have to go. Come on, please."

"We do have to go. But not with you... I was waiting for so long, and it finally happened. Mom came to pick us up."

"Mom." Sammy exclaimed.

"Me and Sammy are going to be with mom now. As we should be. You were never meant to be a father."

"Mom isn't here, Maddy. Please. It's a trick. Stop talking like this. It's not you." I pleaded.

"It is me. But you don't know me, do you? You don't know anything about me. You just use me. You use me to be your housewife because your other housewife left. You don't care how much I hurt."

"That's not true!" I shouted.

"You saw, though, didn't you? I know you saw the scars on my arms. But you pretended you didn't. Because you wanted to keep believing everything was fine. You can't handle when things get tough. You can't handle being a parent. You never should have had us. But it's okay now, dad. Mom's coming to get us. She'll take care of us. You can have your stress-free life."

Tears began to stream down my face. I knew it wasn't really her talking, but I knew she was right about so much. I did see her scars. Deep down, maybe this is how she really felt. If she really had the chance to go be with her mother... maybe she would. Maybe she would have it better over there.

But that's not what this is. This thing was taking from them, and I knew it wouldn't stop. If I get them out of the house, it wouldn't matter. They would continue to be fed upon until they were nothing...

IT TAKES

...Is that what I was? How much had I taken from Maddy all these years? I took her childhood. I took her happiness. I took her dreams. Was I her monster?

It didn't matter anymore. I just had to fix this. This had to end...

And it did.

I don't remember what happened next. All I remember was driving down a long, lonely road with my daughter in the passenger seat and my son asleep in the back. The sun rose in front of us. We were making our way back home.

I may not remember what I did, but I know what I did.

I did what I had to do.

"Where were we?" Maddy asked. "What happened to us, I don't..."

"I fixed it. You're safe now. We're all safe." I said with as much of a smile as I could muster.

"What do you mean? How?" She prodded.

"I love you." I responded, cutting her off. It felt good. I should've said it so much more.

"Eugh." Maddy exclaimed with exaggerated disgust. "Stop."

A few moments passed and then she spoke up again. "Love you too."

After a few days I figured out what it was going to take from me. How smart and insidious it was. Why would it even let me make a bargain like that? It started to make sense.

Little things started to go first. I'd misplace things. I'd reach into my mind to recall something and I would find only fog. That's why I began writing almost right away. Our memories are the most precious things that any of us have, and I don't want mine to die with me.

I am afraid. More afraid than I have ever been. Afraid for the day when I forget more. Afraid for the day when I forget them. Afraid for the day when I'll have to leave them... Until then I'll hold my memories close. As close as I can, for as long as I can. I'll read this book over and over. I will fight to give them everything I have left. I will love them until my last breath. I will remember. That's what you do when you're a parent.

As for why it accepted my bargain, why it chose to take what it did from me... It's obvious. The first thing I forgot was to lock the door on my way out.

IT TAKES

EPILOGUE

MORI

I know what death is. It's not just when your consciousness leaves this earth. Death is so much more. Death is every unsaid thing that can now never be said. Death is every memory remembered for the last time. Death is every little thing you see that reminds you of the person who is supposed to be there, but isn't.

My dad died a thousand times. And I have died a thousand times.

I wish I got to tell you how wrong you were. I wish I got to tell you so many things. There always seemed to be something else in the way.

IT TAKES

You were never my monster. You were never my burden. I never resented you. I never would have left you. You were my dad. That's all. And you were enough.

You always wanted to do the impossible. I think that's what every good parent wants. To win the no-win scenario. To be perfect, and to make our lives perfect. But whether you succeeded or not, never mattered. All that mattered to me was that you tried. And you did, always.

The doctors said the acceleration of his cognitive decline was vicious. They gave him a generous three years before he wouldn't be able to remember anything or anyone.

It took eight years before he forgot my name; and even still, he said he loved me every time he saw me. He fought for us until the end. The last thing I said to him was that me and Sammy were going to be okay. He didn't know us by then, but I still saw his lip curl into a smile.

I wasn't there when he passed. I got the call at 4 a.m. that he was gone. I had said so many final goodbyes, unsure which would be the last, but I still wish I got to be there to say it properly. No one was around to hear if he had any last words. But I know what they were.

One of the few possessions he had to his name was an old CRT. I thought about donating it at first, but something inside me told me to keep it. It sat in my closet after that, but after the first time I read my dad's book, I dug it back out.

I sat it on the floor and plugged it in. I turned it on and sat cross legged in front of it.

Just watching and listening to the static.

I waited, and waited. None of the voices came through as they did before, except one. Only one.

"I remember."

THE END

THE DRUMS
A SHORT STORY

Today feels different. I awake and everything seems a bit hazy. I don't remember what I did the night before. I'm walking outside and all the people I pass by don't have enough detail on them. Neither do the houses. They're like a smear on a lens. Or a painting not yet finished. I don't think I've fully woken up yet.

I don't quite know where I'm going. I don't exactly know where I've been either. All I know is that I have a headache. There's a constant drumbeat echoing in from some place far away. I don't know where it comes from, but I can't escape it.

I know this street but how did I get here? There's my old house, the one I grew up in for 18 years. It's exactly as I remember it, just a little bit foggier. I think something's waiting for me in there, but perhaps I shouldn't impose.

The front door opens and there I see Penelope. My wife, she looks just as beautiful as the first time I saw her – 24 years ago. I remember it vividly; she was standing on a beach a few yards away. Her hair and white sundress blowing in the wind. The sun was in my eyes but I couldn't stop looking. She stood there smiling that same smile and I just knew... And here we are. She hasn't changed a bit. Her smile cuts through the haze. She says I must come inside. Of course I will.

And there's everyone else, all gathered around. This is a surprise party... for me? Is it my birthday? There's my mom, smiling at me just like in the picture above my mantle at home. Pop is here too, although I can't quite make him out. He looks a lot younger than mom, I bet that makes her mad. I wish I had more pictures of him.

My brother and sister are here as well, with their spouses and kids. Its been awhile since I've seen them, we all have our own lives now, but it makes me really happy being together with them again. What are their spouses' names? I can't remember, I feel bad about that... And why don't they have faces?

A pair of arms come around me from behind and interlock and I know exactly whose they are. My little Angie. All the way from college. When she smiles I still see that little girl who would never let us put her in pigtails. I'm so proud of her... But I have to step out. My head is killing me. The drums have been getting louder. Louder or closer, I'm not sure. I need some air. They'll understand.

This is a new street. No. I know this one too. This is where my old apartment was. Before I met Penelope.

That's a blast from the past. My memories feel so close to me. Like fish in a pond and I can just reach out and grab one.

My old roommates Tim and Patty are here, but they also don't have their faces. I wonder what that's about. I want to ask what they've been up to but I don't think they can answer. Oh, and there's my old boss from the restaurant I worked at in college. I wish he didn't have a face. That's one I'd feel better forgetting. What was the restaurant's name? It was something tacky, I remember that.

The swing set at school, so many memories there. Were there two swings or four? If it's two, I'm not going because Drew's on the other one and he makes fun of me. Was it Drew? Who's Drew? The drums are getting louder again.

I'd better get back to the party now. Don't want to worry anyone. Except people are leaving now. I guess it is getting late. I wanted to say goodbye to my brother and sister but they didn't have faces anymore. Pop must've already gone. But my mom is still here. She's leaving too, but she stopped to give me a hug and that made me feel better. Her hugs were the best. I almost forgot what they were like... I'm glad I didn't. Was this the last time I'd feel it? The drums are starting to slow.

Just my wife and daughter now. As it always should be. I wish it could stay this way forever. I would live in this moment. My family. My life. But, my daughter's cab just arrived... It's okay. She has her whole life ahead of her.

She has places to be, things to see. It's okay. I'm so proud of her. She's going to be so great. My Angie.

Please don't go.

Penelope. The love of my life. I'm so glad her face hasn't gone. I can't lose her too. She's still as breathtaking as the first day I saw her, on that beach. But... isn't that today? It must be today. The sun has just about gone over the horizon and it makes the water look perfect.

And there she is, standing right in front of the water in that white sundress. Basking in the glow of the sunset while I bask in the glow of her. The most beautiful girl... If only I knew her name. Maybe I should ask her on a date.

She's looking at me. That smile. I know it from somewhere.

In fact... I think it's all I know. I'm okay with that.

The drums are slowing down. I think there's only one beat left.

"Stay with me." I ask the girl.

"Always."

ACKNOWLEDGMENTS

To my wonderful friends and my amazing partner, you first and foremost made this happen. Your support and love and patience is what keeps me going even in the scariest of times.

To Tay, as always, thank you for being so generous with your feedback, for being such a source of inspiration and aspiration in this silly thing we do, and for just being an awesome friend who has helped change my life for the better. (Check out her new book, 'Something's Wrong With Maddy' by Taylor Z. Adams, it's incredible)

To Hunter and Isaiah, still shooting my shot. That's three shots now and I'm getting a little tired but I can go all night, rest assured.

To Ders, Cozi, Cricket, Tay (again), Scrim, and several other wonderful souls, thank you for helping the K become an A.

And finally to everyone in my beloved horror community who's made me feel welcome and has supported me through all these insane changes—whether you read my stuff or not, thank you so much sickos.

ABOUT THE AUTHOR

From as early as three years old, A.W. Schofield developed a passion for storytelling and the arts. In pre-school, she gravitated toward the easel and never left. In high school, she filled her binders with blank paper in which to write story ideas and draw monsters during any down time they got. Much of her free time, to this day, is still spent writing, drawing, and watching horror movies.

Her ultimate goal in life is simply to tell spooky, emotional, and occasionally gay stories; to provide escapism from the less fun horrors of life. She sees all art as a deeply essential form of human connection, and something that must be protected and kept sacred. She's based in the Greater Toronto Area, but hopes to one day be able to live out her life quietly on the east coast.

Twitter: @schofield_books